Trixie Belden #1
The Secret of the Mansion

by Julie Campbell
illustrated by Mary Stevens
cover illustration by Michael Koelsch

Random House New York

www.randomhouse.com/kids

Library of Congress Cataloging-in-Publication Data
Campbell, Julie, 1908–1999.
The secret of the mansion / by Julie Campbell ; illustrated by Mary Stevens ; cover illustration by Michael Koelsch.
   p. cm. — (Trixie Belden ; #1)
SUMMARY: Thirteen-year-old Trixie Belden and her friends search for hidden treasure in a mysterious mansion owned by an old miser.
ISBN 0-375-82412-X (trade) — ISBN 0-375-92412-4 (lib. bdg.)
[1. Buried treasure—Fiction. 2. Mystery and detective stories.]
I. Stevens, Mary, ill. II. Koelsch, Michael, ill. III. Title. IV. Series.
PZ7.C1547 Se 2003 [Fic]—dc21 2002036990

Printed in the United States of America 10 9 8 7
First Random House Edition

CONTENTS

Chapter 1
The Haunted House

"Oh, Moms," Trixie moaned, running her hands through her short, sandy curls. "I'll just die if I don't have a horse."

Mrs. Belden looked up from the row of tomato plants she was transplanting in the fenced-in vegetable garden.

"Trixie," she said, trying to look stern, "if you died as many times as you thought you were going to, you'd have to be a cat with nine lives to be with us for one day."

"I don't care!" Tears of indignation welled up in Trixie's round blue eyes. She scooped up a fat little worm, watched it wriggle in the palm of her hand for a minute, then gently let it go. "With Brian and Mart at camp this summer, I'll die of boredom. I mean it, Moms."

Mrs. Belden sighed. "You declared you'd suffer the same fate if we didn't buy you a bike three years ago. Remember?" She stood up, frowning in the glare of the hot July sun. "Now listen, Trixie, once and for all. If you want to buy a horse like the one you fell in love with at the horse show yesterday, you will have to earn the money yourself. You know perfectly well the only reason your brothers could go to camp is because they are working as junior counselors."

Crabapple Farm, Trixie reflected, was really a grand place to live, and she had always had a lot of fun there, but she did wish there was another girl in the neighborhood. The big estate, known as the Manor House, which bounded the Belden property on the west had been vacant ever since Trixie could remember. There were no other homes nearby except the crumbling mansion on the eastern hill, where queer old Mr. Frayne lived alone.

The three estates faced a quiet country road two miles from the village of Sleepyside that nestled among the rolling hills on the east bank of the Hudson River. Trixie's father worked in the bank in Sleepyside, and Trixie and her brothers went to the village school. She had many friends in Sleepyside, but she rarely saw them except when school was in session. Now that her brothers, Brian and Mart, had gone to camp, there was nobody but her little brother, Bobby, to play with.

Trixie impatiently kicked a hole in the dust of the path with her shoe.

"It's not fair. You wouldn't let me try for a job as a

waitress or anything. Maybe I could have gone, too."

"You're only thirteen," her mother said patiently. "Next year we might consider something of the sort. Dad and I are really sorry, dear," she added gently, "that we couldn't afford to send you to camp this year."

Trixie suddenly felt ashamed of herself, and she impulsively threw her arms around her mother. "Oh, I know, Moms, and I'm a pest to nag at you. I won't any more. I promise."

"You can begin to earn the money for your horse right here, Trixie," Mrs. Belden said, laughing. "There's plenty to do around here with Brian and Mart away. I'll pay you something every week if you help me with Bobby and the housework. And I know Dad would be glad to increase your allowance if you do some weeding in the garden every day and take over Mart's chore of feeding the chickens and gathering the eggs."

"Oh, Moms!" Trixie hugged her mother tighter. "Maybe I could earn five dollars a week. Do you think I could?"

Mrs. Belden nodded and smiled. "Something like that," she said. "At any rate, if you really work, I should think you could count on having a horse next summer." She shaded her eyes with one hand and stared at the car that was just coming into the driveway. "Why, isn't that

Dad now? What could have happened to bring him home from the bank before lunch?"

Trixie had already darted through the gate and was racing up the path from the vegetable garden, calling over her shoulder, "I'll talk to him right now, and then maybe I can start earning the money for my horse today."

At the top of the driveway, Mr. Belden backed and turned the car around. Trixie jumped on the running board, shouting, "Dad! Mother said I could earn the money for a horse if I help with the garden and chickens and Bobby. May I? Please, Dad, may I?"

Mr. Belden left the motor running but pulled on the emergency brake. "I guess so, Trixie," he said, "but we'll talk about that later. I've just been to the hospital," he spoke to Mrs. Belden as she joined Trixie beside the car. "On my way into the village this morning I found old Mr. Frayne lying at the foot of his driveway. He was unconscious, and I took him right into the hospital."

"Oh, Peter!" Mrs. Belden cried. "That poor old man living up there all alone! I've worried about him so often, but he would never let anyone come near him. He's probably been sick for days."

"That's right," Mr. Belden said. "He's suffering from pneumonia complicated by malnutrition. The doctors said there was very little chance that he would pull through."

"Serves him right," Trixie said, wiping her grimy hands on her rolled-up blue jeans. "The mean old miser. You should have left him lying in the driveway, Dad."

Mr. Belden frowned. "Why, Trixie! I don't like you to talk that way, and you know you don't mean it. Although Mr. Frayne may not have always been a very pleasant neighbor, he is still a neighbor."

"I'm sorry, Dad." Trixie squinted up at the big rambling mansion half-hidden by the trees on top of the hill. "He never seemed like a neighbor to me," she added under her breath.

As her father drove away, she turned to her mother. "Why, old man Frayne said he'd call the police if he ever caught any of us trespassing. Remember that time he yelled at Mart and—?"

"Now, Trixie," Mrs. Belden interrupted. "You're old enough to understand Mr. Frayne's attitude. He and your father had a disagreement about the boundary line between the two properties. Of course, Dad didn't want to take the matter to court because nobody really cares who owns that little patch of the woods, but Mr. Frayne insisted. Naturally, when the decision went against him he resented it."

Trixie pulled up a piece of grass and chewed it

thoughtfully. "Well, his game chickens come down on our property whenever they please, and you don't complain. And just last week, Moms, Reddy chased Queenie, the black hen, into Mr. Frayne's property. I tore after him because I didn't want him to hurt Queenie, even though she does belong to the old miser. But I needn't have worried, because I guess those game hens can take care of themselves. Just as I caught up to them, she suddenly turned and flew right into Reddy's face, flapping her wings and squawking and scratching like anything." Trixie laughed. "Reddy was the most surprised Irish setter you ever saw. He tucked his tail between his legs and dashed off into the woods, and just then Mr. Frayne burst out of his house, waving a shotgun and shouting at me. Golly, I was awfully scared for a minute, Moms. He said he'd shoot Reddy if he ever crossed the boundary line again."

"I'm sorry that happened, dear," Mrs. Belden said as they strolled back to the garden. "But I honestly don't think Mr. Frayne would really shoot Reddy."

"I do." Trixie kicked a pebble across the path. "He's such a wrinkled little old man with such a cross face. I bet he doesn't weigh much more than Bobby does, and in those funny, patched clothes, he looks like a scarecrow. And his land's in a terrible state. It's all choked with weeds and vines except for a clearing right around the house which isn't a lawn any more, because the chickens have scratched it bare."

"He wasn't always a wrinkled old man, Trixie," Mrs. Belden said quietly. "And Ten Acres was once as much of a showplace as the Manor House on the other hill is now. Grief sometimes changes people, you know. Before Mrs. Frayne died, he was a charming old gentleman, and he and his wife were very kind to your father and me when we moved up here from the city. That was before you were born, and Brian and Mart were still babies." She carefully slipped a cardboard collar around one of the tomato plants. "I'll never forget the night Mrs. Frayne died. It was a terrible shock to all of us."

"What happened, Mother?" Trixie knelt in the next row and began thinning the feathery little carrots. "All I know is that she was bitten by a copperhead snake. But you don't *have* to die from a copperhead bite. Dad told us all long ago what to do in case any of us were bitten. First, you put on a tourniquet; then you cut into the fang marks with a knife or a razor blade, and then you suck out the blood to keep the poison from spreading. Didn't Mr. Frayne know what to do, Moms?"

Mrs. Belden pressed the last tomato plant into place with her fingers and stood up.

"I don't know, Trixie, but he must have been terribly upset. He absolutely adored his wife. She was a beautiful little old lady, and everyone loved her." She slipped off her gloves and wiped her face with her handkerchief. "It happened one evening when they were sitting out in their summerhouse. The snake must have been curled under Mrs. Frayne's chair, and she probably kicked it accidentally. When Mrs. Frayne cried out, Mr. Frayne just picked her up in his arms to rush her to the hospital for the antivenin. Naturally, he took the short cut, and right in the middle of that deserted upper road, the car broke down. Whether he didn't know what to do, or was too excited to do anything, I do not know. At any rate, they simply waited there until a car came along. They waited for hours, and, by that time, it was too late."

"How dreadful, Moms," Trixie gasped.

Shading her eyes with her hand, Mrs. Belden glanced up at the old mansion on the eastern hill.

"Poor Mr. Frayne," she murmured. "He was never the same again. He left his car right there on the road where it had broken down and never allowed another automobile on the place after that." She added slowly, "I wonder what happened to the summerhouse. You used to be able to see it quite plainly from here."

But Trixie was no longer looking at the Frayne mansion. She was looking in the opposite direction.

"Moms, Moms!" she cried. "Something's going on up at the Manor House. See all those vans? Somebody must be moving in."

Mrs. Belden turned and glanced up at the huge estate which bounded Crabapple Farm on the west.

"Why, yes, Trixie," she said. "I meant to tell you last night, but you were too excited about that horse to listen. A family named Wheeler moved in yesterday. Your father met Mr. Wheeler at the bank. He has a daughter about your age and told Dad he hoped you'd run up and see her."

"Oh, Mother," Trixie interrupted excitedly. "Do you see what I see? Horses! Horses being led out toward the stables. Couldn't I go up right now and meet Mr. Wheeler's daughter?"

Mrs. Belden smiled. "Well, I guess it's all right. But what about your job?"

Trixie saw her little brother racing across the lawn with Reddy at his heels.

"I'll take Bobby with me," she said quickly, "so you won't have to worry about him. Come on, Bobby, hurry up." Trixie pulled open the gate so hard she almost tore it off its hinges.

"Hey!" Bobby shouted as he started down the path to the gate. "Where're you going? Can I go, too? Wait for me, Trixie."

The middle of the path was rough with partially exposed tree roots, and Bobby tripped, as he often did, and sprawled in the red-brown dust. Trixie stared at him with disgust. "Oh, Bobby, Bobby," she cried, "now you're all dirty. You can't go calling on rich people looking like that!"

Bobby scrambled to his feet, rubbing the dirt into his moist skin as he tried to brush it off. "Hey!" He grinned. "What rich people? Do I look all right now, Trixie? I wanna go calling on rich people."

Trixie turned to her mother in despair. "Do I have to take him, Mother? Do I *have* to?"

Mrs. Belden shrugged her shoulders. "That depends on whether or not you feel a horse is worth working for. You could, of course, finish thinning the carrots instead, and there's an hour's dusting to do indoors."

"Oh, all right, Moms." Trixie grabbed Bobby's grimy hand. She was tired of working in the garden, and she despised any kind of housework. "But first I'll wash you up," she told the little boy, "and put a clean sunsuit on you. And for heaven's sake, Bobby, when you

meet these people, don't tell them I said they were rich, and please try to stop yelling 'Hey' all the time."

Ten minutes later, Trixie and Bobby began the long climb up the Manor House driveway with Reddy racing ahead of them. At the turn in the road, a fat little cocker spaniel rushed down to meet them. Right behind the puppy was a tall thin girl whose pale face was framed in shoulder-length, light-brown hair. She cringed as Reddy, disdainfully ignoring the black puppy, raced around her in circles, barking furiously.

"Don't pay any attention to him," Trixie cried quickly, seeing that her new neighbor was really frightened. "He's just showing off. He wouldn't hurt a fly. I'm Trixie Belden," she went on hurriedly. "My kid brother and I live in the hollow in that little white frame house— Crabapple Farm, you know."

The girl stared solemnly from Trixie to Bobby and back again. "How do you do?" she said, holding out her slender hand. "My name is Honey—Honey Wheeler."

Trixie shook hands, feeling rather foolish at such a display of formality. *Oh, my,* she thought, almost sick with disappointment, *she's stuck-up. Who would go around in a white linen dress and stockings and sandals unless there's a party?* Aloud she asked, without much hope, "Do you ride horseback?"

Honey smiled, then. "Oh, yes," she said. "Do you?"

Trixie shook her head ruefully. "No, but I want to learn like anything. The only thing I have to ride is a babyish old bike. But I'm earning the money now to buy a horse just as soon as I can."

"A bike?" Honey's smile widened, and Trixie had to admit that the girl was really pretty in a pale sort of way. "I wish I had a bike," she said wistfully. "Mother wouldn't let me have one in the city because of traffic, and the rest of the time I was at boarding school and camp where they're not allowed." Timidly she moved a step nearer to Trixie. "I'll teach you how to ride horseback," she offered. "Then perhaps you would show me how to ride a bike."

Trixie could hardly believe her ears. "That's great," she gasped. "Let's start right away. I mean the horseback part. I can teach you how to ride a bike any time." She turned impatiently to Bobby, who was joyously cuddling the cocker spaniel puppy. "You go home now, Bobby, and play in the sandpile."

Bobby ignored her and grinned up at Honey. "Are you rich?" he demanded. "Hey! What's it like to be rich?"

Trixie felt her cheeks flame hotly, but Honey merely smiled and said, "It's not nice at all, Bobby. I can't remember when I didn't want to be like other people." She turned shyly toward Trixie and added, "When I was little, my nurses never let me play in the dirt the way Bobby is now, and I was never allowed to go any place by myself for fear of being kidnaped." She stopped suddenly as her enormous hazel eyes filled with tears. "I hardly ever saw my father and mother until I got sick. And now they've bought this big old place just for me. But what good is it? What good is anything if you're never allowed to have any fun?"

Trixie could never bear to see anyone unhappy. "Gee," she said, putting her arm sympathetically around Honey's thin shoulders. "I never thought about it like that. I always thought it would be wonderful to have a lot of money." She stopped as the word *money* gave her an idea. "I tell you what let's do." She whirled Honey around and pointed across the woods to Ten Acres, which she called Miser's Mansion in her own mind. "See that big old gray and yellow house on the opposite hill?"

Honey nodded and dabbed at her eyes with a dainty handkerchief.

"Well," Trixie went on excitedly, "a crazy old man lives there all alone. Dad took him to the hospital this morning, so this is a swell time to explore. I've always wanted to see what the inside of the house was like."

"Trixie Belden!" Honey gasped in a shocked voice.

"You wouldn't really break into somebody's house!"

"Of course not." Trixie grinned. "Old Mr. Frayne would probably have me thrown in jail if I did such a thing. But there's no reason why we couldn't peek in through a window. You know what they say in the village?" she demanded. "They say there's a half million dollars hidden there. Let's go!"

"I wouldn't go near that creepy old place," Honey said firmly. "And I don't believe there's any money hidden there. Why, the house is practically falling to pieces, and it hasn't been painted in ages."

"How do you know all that?" Trixie demanded impatiently. "You can't see it *that* clearly from here."

"I was there early this morning," Honey explained. "Daddy and I were out riding, and we went up that old driveway thinking it was a road to the woods. We didn't realize that it led to the Mansion until we were halfway up. Then, of course, we knew we were trespassing, so we turned around. It looked like a deserted house to me, and I was glad to get away from there. Nobody would want to live in such a horrible, run-down place."

Trixie bent down and fumbled with her shoelace to hide the disappointment on her face. *She's worse than I thought she was at first,* she thought. *A silly old fraidy cat.* Aloud she said coldly, "Of course, a lot of people think old Mr. Frayne went crazy after his wife died, and he lost all his money. That's why the place is run-down. Anyway, I'm going to look around there while Mr. Frayne's in the hospital. You don't have to if you don't want to."

"Are you sure he's in the hospital?" Honey asked, suddenly.

Trixie straightened up. "Of course. Dad took him in early this morning. He's not expected to live."

"That's funny," Honey said slowly. "We were there about an hour ago. As we rode down the hill, I got the creepy feeling you get when you know somebody you can't see is watching you. I looked back over my shoulder quickly, and I saw a face at one of the windows." She shivered slightly. "I'll bet that house is haunted!"

Chapter 2
Through the Hedge

Trixie hooted with laughter. "You're just imagining things," she said. "I never heard of anything so silly."

Honey bit her lip. "Naturally, I don't really believe in ghosts," she said in a hurt voice, "but I did see a face at the window."

"Oh, skip it," Trixie said impatiently. "If you're really scared, I'll explore up there myself some other time. Right now, I can hardly wait to get on a horse." She gave Honey a little push. "Go on and change into dungarees."

Honey stared at her. "I haven't any dungarees," she said slowly. "I always wear a habit and boots when I ride."

"What difference does it make what you wear?" Trixie interrupted. She wheeled around to where Bobby was rolling in the grass with the puppy. "Go on home now," she wheedled. "If you're a good boy this morning, I'll play with you all afternoon. It's a promise."

Bobby giggled as the puppy licked his face. "Don't want to go home. Want to stay here and play with the puppy. Hey, what's his name, anyway?" he asked Honey.

"Bud." Honey smiled. "Bobby doesn't have to go home, Trixie," she said quietly. "He can stay here with my governess. Miss Trask won't mind keeping an eye on him. She's really very nice, you know. She's not like the other ones who were perfectly horrible. Oh, here she comes now."

Around the bend in the driveway appeared a trim, middle-aged woman with very short, crisp, gray hair. She was wearing a tailored slack suit and sturdy-looking brown and white oxfords. She had bright blue eyes which twinkled merrily as she caught sight of Bobby frolicking with the puppy.

"What have we here?" she asked with a friendly smile. "So you've found some playmates already, Honey?"

"Oh, yes," Honey cried. "This is Trixie Belden and her brother, Bobby. They live in that darling little farmhouse down in the hollow. We were just about to go riding."

Trixie, slightly awed in the presence of such an unknown creature as a governess, mumbled, "How do you do?"

Bobby scrambled to his feet. "Hey," he shouted, tossing his silky curls in Honey's direction. "*She* said you'd keep an eye on me while they 'splore. Trixie's supposed to, you know, instead of weeding, but I won't tell if you play games with me."

Trixie felt like shaking the little boy, but Miss Trask held out her hand to him, laughing. "Of course, I'll play games with you. Run along, Honey, and have a nice ride through the woods with your new friend." She glanced approvingly at Trixie's dungarees. "It's a pity you have to bother to change, Honey," she said. "Now that we're in the country, you really ought to dress the way Trixie does. I'll speak to your mother right away about getting you some blue jeans and loafers."

Honey threw her arms impulsively around her governess. "Oh, Miss Trask, will you? You're such an angel. And will you also ask her if I can have a bike, too? Trixie's going to teach me how to ride one. I've wanted a bike ever since I can remember." She ran off toward the house, her pale face flushed with pleasure.

Trixie stared after her, thinking, *Why, she's just like a poor little rich girl in a storybook. Imagine having to ask your governess to ask your mother for something! It's no wonder she acts so queer, sometimes.*

Miss Trask turned to Trixie as Honey went into the house to change. As though reading Trixie's mind, Miss Trask said quietly, "It's truly shameful the way that child has been brought up. I mean to see to it that a lot of changes are made. She has just recovered from a long illness and is still rather nervous. I'd like her to get as tanned and strong as you are. Will you help me, Trixie?"

Trixie looked down at the toe of her shoe, embarrassed. "Why, sure," she said huskily. "I don't know exactly what you mean, Miss Trask, but I'll help. Of course I will."

"Good." Miss Trask swung Bobby's hand as they strolled up the sloping driveway and back to the newly white-washed stable where tall stalks of pink and red hollyhocks grew in profusion. A broad-shouldered, pleasant-faced man was grooming a big black horse, and Miss Trask called out to him.

"Good morning, Regan. This is Miss Trixie Belden. Will you saddle a couple of horses, so she and Honey can explore the woods?" She smiled at Trixie. "Have fun. Don't worry about Bobby. I'll let him play in the wading pool until you come back."

"Thanks," Trixie said, staring entranced at the big gleaming horse. She sucked in a deep breath of the air that was fragrant with the smell of clean horses and hay and saddle soap. She moved closer and patted the gelding's satiny neck. "Oh, you beautiful, beautiful thing," she crooned as Jupiter nuzzled her pocket, hinting for a lump of sugar. "I haven't anything for you today, darling, but tomorrow I'll bring you apples and carrots. Just you wait and see."

"You speak a horse's language, Miss," Regan said approvingly. "Jupe understood every word you said. He likes you and he doesn't like everybody."

"I *love* him," Trixie cried. "Please, Mr. Regan, could I ride him today?"

"Well, now," Regan said slowly, "that depends. He's not easy to handle, Jupiter isn't. Mr. Wheeler rides him mostly, and he's got a very heavy touch. Honey now, she can't hold Jupiter in. Just hasn't enough strength in her wrists. But you look like a husky youngster. Done much riding?"

Reluctantly, Trixie shook her head. "I've never even been on a horse," she admitted ruefully. "But I know I can ride him, Mr. Regan. I *know* I can."

Regan guffawed loudly. "Never even been on a horse! Why, Miss, you wouldn't have a chance in the world with Jupe. He'd know right off that you were a beginner, and would he take you for a ride!" He slapped Jupiter's neck affectionately. "He wouldn't stop until you hit the New York traffic; that is, if you stayed on that long."

Trixie swallowed hard to keep from showing her disappointment. "But when I learn to ride, you'll let me try him, won't you, Mr. Regan?" she begged meekly. "Please!"

"That I will," Regan promised. "But, right now, I think you'd better start with Lady. She's real gentle and easy to handle. Mrs. Wheeler's mare, she is. Come on, you can help me saddle her."

Trixie followed him inside the stable, and a lovely dapple-gray mare whinnied from her stall. "That's the sweet girl," Regan crooned as he slipped a halter over Lady's head and led her out. "Here, Miss," he said to Trixie, "you hold her a minute," and he disappeared into the tack room.

The horsy smell of leather and soap and hay was stronger in here, and Trixie inhaled a deep breath of it as she waited for Regan. "You're a darling girl," she whispered to the dainty little mare, "and I wish you belonged to me." When Regan came back, she said, "Please don't call me Miss, Mr. Regan. My name's Trixie."

Regan deftly slid the halter over Lady's head and slipped a snaffle bit into her mouth. "Okay, Trixie," he said as he showed her how to gather up the reins. "Just call me Regan." He gently placed a saddle on Lady's back and bent over to buckle the girth in place. "I'll have to tighten the cinch a bit after you get on," he told Trixie.

"Lady has the habit of blowing herself up while she's being saddled." He grinned. "It's a smart trick, and you have to watch out for it with a lot of horses. Wouldn't want the saddle to slip off, would you?"

Trixie solemnly shook her head. Regan led Lady out into the yard and pulled down the stirrups. Measuring the length of Trixie's leg with his eye, he adjusted the leather straps accordingly. He held one stirrup iron for her. "Up you go," he ordered.

Trixie promptly discovered that mounting a horse was not as easy as she had thought it would be; but after two unsuccessful tries she found herself, breathless and excited, in the saddle. She was on a horse at last!

"Heels down!" Regan commanded. "And keep 'em down, with the irons under the balls of your feet." He led Lady into a partially fenced-in field. "If you don't keep your heels down, you'll never learn how to post a trot or keep your seat in a gallop. What's more, if you get thrown and the horse runs away, you're not likely to have your foot caught in a stirrup if your heels are down instead of your toes. Getting dragged isn't fun," he finished soberly. "Just remember that!"

"I will," Trixie promised, so thrilled that her whole body trembled. "May I gallop her now, Regan, may I?"

"Indeed you don't," Regan said briskly. "You start

with a walk. Just lift the reins a little, and she'll move right out."

Honey appeared, then, in an immaculate white riding habit and russet boots so shiny you could see your face in them. "Come here, Honey," Regan said. "Lead your friend around the corral a couple of times while I saddle Strawberry. Trixie'd better get the feel of the saddle a bit before she gets too frisky."

Trixie tried to control her impatience as they walked around the field, and Honey asked, "Are you really going up to that old mansion?"

"Sure," Trixie said. "Why don't we ride through the woods right now? You don't have to go way up to the house if you don't want to."

Honey thought about this for a minute, and then she said, "All right. I guess I was mistaken about that face. I do imagine things, you know, such weird things."

"Everybody does," Trixie said good-naturedly. "When I was a kid, whenever there was a thunderstorm, I thought I saw the headless horseman galloping across the sky in the flashes of lightning."

Honey stopped and looked up at her curiously. "Headless horseman?" she repeated, in a surprised voice. "How awful!"

Trixie grinned. "Sure, this is the part of the Hudson

River Valley that Washington Irving wrote about in *The Legend of Sleepy Hollow*. The village got its name, Sleepyside, from that old story, you know."

"Oh." Honey looked relieved, but she added seriously, "I hope I don't dream about a headless horseman. I have awful nightmares, sometimes. I wake up screaming."

"Do I have to keep on walking Lady, forever?" Trixie interrupted impatiently.

"I guess you could try trotting, now," Honey said. "Gather up the reins a little and touch Lady's flank lightly with one heel."

Lady obediently set off at a smooth trot, but Trixie bounced and jounced in the saddle until she thought her head would jar off. *That would make the legend come true. I'd be a headless horseman,* she thought grimly. She could not keep her feet in the stirrups, and the swinging irons hit Lady's sides sharply. Thinking Trixie wanted her to go faster, Lady broke into a canter. Before Trixie knew what had happened, she was lying in the middle of the field, staring forlornly up at the bright blue sky. She wasn't the least bit hurt, but she winced inwardly. *Now's Honey's chance to get back at me for making fun of her when she thought she saw a face at the Mansion,* she reflected bitterly.

She scrambled to her feet and was surprised to see

that Honey, who was calmly holding Lady's head, was not laughing. "Everybody does that the first time, Trixie," she said. "Anyway, I'm glad you're not hurt."

Trixie meekly climbed back into the saddle. "I was an awful dope," she said. "I didn't keep my heels down. I'll do better next time."

Regan came into the corral then, leading a magnificent strawberry roan called Strawberry. Regan left Honey to mount without his help; and Trixie noticed, with envy, that although Strawberry tossed his head and pranced, Honey seemed to have no difficulty and adjusted her own stirrups from her seat in the saddle.

"Regan," Trixie breathed admiringly, "do you think I'll ever get that good?"

"Sure." Regan stared at the grass stains on Trixie's shirt and then said with a little note of amusement and understanding in his voice, "Had your first spill already, huh?"

Trixie nodded shamefacedly.

"Well, now, you know what I think?" Regan demanded. "I think you ought to take it easy this first day. Mrs. Wheeler rode Lady this morning before breakfast, so the mare doesn't need any more exercise. Why don't you just keep her at a walk until you sort of get used to things?" He added quickly as Trixie's face

32

showed her disappointment, "I'll give you a lesson in posting tomorrow. You'll catch on quick, don't worry. People who really love horses are just natural-born riders."

"I think Regan's right," Honey said. "If you do too much today, Trixie, you'll be so stiff tomorrow you won't even be able to climb into a saddle, much less ride."

"But I'll spoil your fun," Trixie objected. "You'll want to trot and canter and I won't be able to keep up."

Honey smiled. "It's awfully hot, anyway, and Strawberry will work himself into a lather if I let him out of a walk. I can exercise him this evening when it's cooler."

Golly, Trixie thought, *she is a good sport. She just said that to make it easier for me.* Aloud, she said with a grin, "Okay, Honey, you're the boss at this ranch."

They walked their horses along the path that circled the willow-bordered lake, and Trixie saw a new rowboat tied alongside the rustic boathouse. "Oh, boy!" she shouted. "Now we can fish in the middle of the lake. You're a lucky duck to live up here, Honey!"

"I don't know how to fish," Honey said quickly. "And I wouldn't touch a horrible squirming worm for anything!"

The word "Sissy!" was on the tip of Trixie's tongue,

but she caught herself just in time. "I'll put the worms on the hook," she said. "We can have a lot of fun. Brian and Mart and I have caught a lot of fish off the boathouse. You see," she explained, "the Manor House has been empty for so many years we got so we thought of the lake as belonging to our property."

"I want you to keep right on thinking that, Trixie," Honey cried impulsively. "You and your brothers must come here as often as you like."

"Great," Trixie said. "We can skate on it in winter and toboggan down your hill." They were in the woods now and Trixie added, "I can hardly wait to see what it's like inside the Miser's Mansion. I've always wanted to know whether he really is a miser or just a poor old grouch."

"It looks as though the house had been empty for years," Honey said as they approached the Frayne property. "Why, the upstairs windows are so covered with dirt you can't see through them. And just look at the way everything has grown up around here. It's a regular wilderness except for that little space right around the house."

The trail ended at the boundary line between the two properties which was marked by a thick hedge interlaced with heavy vines. A narrow path wound from this point down the hill to the hollow and Crabapple Farm.

"Let's tie our horses to this tree," Trixie said as she slid out of the saddle, "and push our way through the hedge. If we go around to the driveway, somebody might see us and wonder what we're doing."

"I wouldn't dare crawl through that underbrush," Honey said as she dismounted. "It's probably alive with snakes."

Trixie paid no attention to her and started through the hedge. "Wonder whatever happened to the summerhouse where Mrs. Frayne got bitten by the copperhead," she said, tugging at a ropelike vine. "It must have been right about here if Mother could see it plainly from the garden down in the hollow."

"Copperhead!" Honey had forced herself to take a few steps after Trixie, but now she stopped, shaking with horror. "Are there copperheads around here?"

"Sure," Trixie shrugged. "But they won't hurt you unless you bother them."

"I can't stand snakes," Honey insisted, with a shiver. "And copperheads are poisonous. I wouldn't want to be bitten by one of them."

"You won't be bitten, Honey," Trixie assured her, pushing ahead.

"I'm not so sure of that." Honey cringed as a vine

slapped against her face. "Didn't you just say that Mrs. Frayne got bitten?"

"That was in the summerhouse," Trixie said. "And the summerhouse seems to have disappeared. Anyway, it was one of those things that happen once in a lifetime."

"Once is enough," Honey said with a nervous giggle as she gingerly took another step forward. At that moment, the underbrush sprang to life as a loud squawking sound rent the silence, and something black and angry flapped against Honey's legs. Honey screamed in terror and frantically grabbed Trixie's arm.

Chapter 3
A Scream and a Dog

Trixie was so startled herself that, for a moment, she stood stock-still. Then, she laughed with relief as she saw that their attacker was Queenie, the little black game hen. With Honey still clinging to her arm, Trixie shouted, "Come on!" and pushed the rest of the way into the clearing. Queenie flung herself at Honey's legs once more, then, squawking like an irate fury, darted across the courtyard. The other hens immediately took up the chorus, fluttering and cackling in wild confusion as they scattered in all directions. From the safety of the woods on the other side of the house, the bright-colored game cock flapped his wings and crowed defiantly.

"What was it?" Honey asked weakly. "I never was so scared in all my life."

"Nothing but a little black hen," Trixie said. "Why, you're shaking like a leaf. I was kind of scared myself," she admitted. "In another minute, she would have flown in our faces. It was a good thing you had boots on. She would have scratched your legs plenty."

"Oh, please, Trixie," Honey pleaded. "Let's go

home. She may come back any minute."

Trixie burst into laughter. "Don't be such a fraidy cat, Honey. She wouldn't have come near us if she hadn't thought we were after her eggs. She must have a nest somewhere around here, and she won't come near this spot again for a long time for fear we might find where it's hidden."

She led the way across the clearing. "Come on, let's peek through a window." Honey followed reluctantly.

There was something so gloomy and forbidding about the weatherbeaten old house that even Trixie found herself whispering as they approached it. The downstairs windows were almost as dirty as the upstairs ones, and she had to wipe a spot on the glass in order to peer inside. "Honey," she said, "this must have been the dining-room, once. Look at that sideboard—it's white with mold, and did you ever see so much junk in all your life?"

The room was piled high with yellowed news-papers, tin cans, and cardboard cartons of every de-scription. Stacked on the sideboard, table, and chairs were dirty bottles and jars of all sizes and shapes.

"I'll bet all those boxes and cans and jars are full of money," Trixie said in an awed voice. "I wish we dared go inside."

Honey shuddered. "I wouldn't go in there for anything in the world. It's probably full of spiders and rats. And this is the very window where I saw a face early this morning."

Trixie stared thoughtfully. "Did you really and truly see someone, Honey? Are you sure you weren't just imagining?"

"Cross my heart and hope to die," Honey said. "Someone or some*thing* was staring at Daddy and me as we rode away."

"It might have been a tramp," Trixie said slowly. "And one way to find out is to see if any of the doors or windows are unlocked. If they are, we ought to lock them to make sure nobody breaks in here while Mr. Frayne is in the hospital."

She ran up the rickety front steps, which sagged dangerously beneath her weight, and twisted the doorknob back and forth. "That's locked," she said as she jumped off the porch. "Let's check the windows."

The front windows were all either locked or warped out of shape, but the first one Trixie tried on the east side of the house opened rather easily. "I'll have to go in and lock it from the inside," she said, climbing over the ledge.

"Then how will you get out again?" Honey demanded.

"The key to the back door is probably in the lock," Trixie said. "After I've checked all the windows, I'll let myself out that way, then lock the back door from the outside and give Dad the key to keep for Mr. Frayne. Come on in and help me."

"I don't think we ought to go in," Honey said nervously. "As you said yourself, it's against the law."

"I'm not breaking any law," Trixie said exasperatedly. "I'm only doing what any neighbor would do for another. If Mr. Frayne were conscious, he'd probably ask us to make sure his house was all locked up."

Something scuttled across the floor as Trixie jumped down from the window sill. "Nothing but a field mouse," she told Honey, with a mischievous grin. "He's more scared of us than you are of him. But you'd better climb inside. That hen might come back any minute."

Honey glanced fearfully over her shoulder. "I guess you're right," she said. "It wouldn't be neighborly to leave the place unlocked." She swung herself gingerly through the window. "But suppose that face I saw belonged to a tramp," she whispered. "And suppose the tramp is still here?"

Trixie shrugged. "Then we'll tell him to get out or we'll call the police. Come on, let's be sure the key is in the back door before we check the windows."

This room, which had once been the luxurious study, was as cluttered as the dining-room. The pictures and prints on the walls were thickly coated with dust, and a barricade of barrels blocked the other windows. The huge roll-top desk was fuzzy with mold, and mice had obviously been nesting in the upholstery of the leather-covered sofa. A green fly droned monotonously against a windowpane, but there was no other sound to break the eerie, empty silence of the old house. It was like the threatening hush that comes before a thunderstorm. The girls picked their way across the room, walking on tiptoe, hardly daring to whisper. At the entrance to the next room, Trixie stopped with a gasp of surprise.

The enormous paneled living-room was filled with debris, and lying sound asleep on an old mattress in the middle of the floor was a tall, redheaded boy. Close beside him was a shotgun, and near his head was a silver christening mug that gleamed in the sunlight which poured in through an open window.

Honey pointed a trembling finger at the boy. "That must be the face I saw this morning," she whispered.

Trixie looked at her blankly. "At least, it wasn't a ghost," she giggled. "But who in the world can he be? He must be about Brian's age—fifteen, don't you think?"

Honey nodded. "I'm scared. Suppose he wakes up

and finds us here? He might shoot us with that awful-looking gun."

Trixie was not at all sure that the boy wouldn't do just that, but she took a cautious step forward, hoping to read the inscription on the silver mug. The floor board creaked suddenly, startling her so that she lost her balance and clutched at the stack of mildewed books. The pile swayed for a minute in midair, then the books toppled to the floor with a loud crash.

The girls stood frozen in their tracks as the boy woke up in a flash and grabbed the gun. There was no sign of friendliness on the boy's freckled face, and his green eyes were dark with suspicion.

Honey found her voice first. "Oh, please, don't shoot us," she almost sobbed. "We didn't mean to spy on you. Really we didn't."

The boy frowned and set his jaw. "What are you doing here?" he demanded sullenly. "You have no business in this house."

Trixie came out of her shocked trance then. "Neither have you," she said hotly. "This place belongs to Mr. James Winthrop Frayne, our neighbor. My father took him to the hospital this morning. We were just checking to be sure all the doors and windows were locked. But you," she finished tartly, "seem to have moved right in."

The boy got slowly to his feet, still clutching the gun. "To the hospital?" he repeated dazedly. "Where and why?"

"The Sleepyside Hospital," Trixie told him. "He's got pneumonia and he's half-starved, too. Not," she added, "that it's any of your business, but the doctors don't think he'll get well."

The boy's broad shoulders drooped disconsolately as he carefully laid the gun on the mattress at his heels. "I thought he was dead," he said, more to himself than to the girls. "When I got here this morning and found the place deserted and filled with junk, I figured Uncle James must have died a long time ago."

"Uncle James!" Trixie and Honey stared at him, wide-eyed. "Was—is—Mr. Frayne your uncle?"

For answer the boy reached down and picked up the silver cup. He held it out so that Trixie could see the engraving. She read the words out loud in an astonished voice: "James Winthrop Frayne II."

"My great-uncle," the boy explained. "I walked most of the way from Albany to find him. But I guess I got here too late." He shrugged. "Well, I'll stick around for a while, anyway. There's a vegetable garden in the back and plenty of chickens and rabbits and squirrels. And," he went on in a sullen, threatening voice, "if you girls tell anyone I'm here, I'll fix you good."

"We're not tattletales," Trixie cried indignantly in protest.

"But what about your father and mother?" Honey asked. "Won't they worry about you?"

"I haven't any family except Uncle James," the boy told her in a still more sullen voice. "I've got a stepfather, if you can call him that. I call him Simon Legree, myself. And if he finds out where I am, he'll drag me back to his farm and beat me and make me slave from morning till night without pay." Tensely, he wound his strong fingers around the silver mug. "I tell you, I won't go back and nobody's going to make me. See?"

Timidly, almost tearfully, Honey burst out with: "Of course you don't have to go back. You can come home and live with my family. My father'll adopt you. I've always wanted a brother, and Daddy's got lots of money so you can have a horse and a dog and anything else you want. Nobody'll ever beat you again."

"Don't be silly," Trixie interrupted. "He can stay at our house where he'll have brothers about the same age. I've got three of them," she grinned. "The youngest one is an awful pest, but Brian and Mart are swell. And my mother and father are just wonderful."

The boy laughed sarcastically. "Gee, you two are

45

funny," he sneered. "Arguing about who's going to have me. Stop your kidding! One would think you really meant it."

"I do mean it," Trixie and Honey cried together, and then they laughed, too.

"I believe you do," he said, sobering slowly, and all of the tense stubbornness seemed to ebb out of him. "Nobody's been nice to me since my mother died two years ago, and I guess I've forgotten how to act with decent people." He held out his right hand. "Shake," he said. "My name's Jim. What's yours?"

Solemnly, the girls shook hands with him in turn and introduced themselves.

"I'm Trixie Belden, and I live down there at Crabapple Farm," Trixie said.

"And I'm Honey Wheeler, and I just moved into the large house on the hill," Honey added.

"Well," Jim said, "I'd sure like to be adopted by both of you, but it's impossible. Jonesy—that's my step-father—is my legal guardian, and he'll never let any-body take his place. You see," he went on as the three of them sat down on the old mattress, "when I was born, my father's Uncle James sent me this mug; and at the same time, he wrote Mother and Dad that he and Aunt Nell were naming me in their wills as their sole heir.

Shortly after that Aunt Nell died, and Mother never heard from him again; but she always told me that some day I'd inherit about half a million dollars, and Jonesy thinks he's going to have control of it when Uncle James dies." He glanced ruefully around the cluttered room. "It looks like I'm going to inherit nothing but a lot of old junk, doesn't it?"

"Don't be too sure of that," Trixie cried excitedly. "A lot of people think there's a fortune hidden in this old house."

"That's impossible, Trixie," Honey declared emphatically. "Nobody who had any money would live in such an untidy place."

"That's right," Jim agreed. "Uncle James must have lost all his money in bad investments. But Jonesy doesn't think so. You see, he snooped around in Sleepyside right after Mother died and heard the same story that there's a fortune in this old mansion, somewhere. He's just waiting until Uncle James dies so he can get his hands on it. I'll never see a penny of it."

"He sounds like an awful person," Honey said, tears of sympathy welling up in her hazel eyes. "Did he really beat you, Jim?"

"Sure," Jim said nonchalantly. "But I didn't mind that so much. Of course, he never did while Mother was alive. He really loved her, and I guess she loved him. She was never very strong," he continued, his green eyes dark with sorrow, "and Jonesy was always very gentle with her. I hated him from the beginning, and I know he felt the same way about me; but we never let Mother know how we felt. It would have broken her heart."

Trixie didn't dare look at Honey, because she knew she would burst into tears if she did. "Is your father dead, too, Jim?" she asked quietly.

"Yes." He stared out of the window for a minute, and the sun glinted in the gold lights in his bright red hair. "You know what?" he asked suddenly. "Some day, I'm going to own a great big all-year-round camp for kids who haven't any fathers of their own. I'm going to run it so they can study lessons and learn a trade at the same time that I teach them how to swim and box and shoot and ride and skate. They're going to know how to live in the woods and understand all kinds of wild animals. My dad taught me to—" He stopped, his freckled face flushed with embarrassment. "I guess this sounds pretty funny to you. Me shooting off like this in a broken-down old house without even a cent to my name!"

"It doesn't sound funny at all!" Trixie broke in. "It sounds great. I bet you will do it some day, too, Jim."

"I bet you do, too," Honey echoed. "I'd like to go to

a camp like that instead of the dull ones I went to."

Jim spread his hands hopelessly. "Well, I've got a long way to go. That's what Jonesy and I fought about mostly. Last summer and this, I wanted to apply at one of those big, upstate boys' camps for a job as junior counselor or junior athletic instructor. I'm pretty good at most sports, and when Dad was alive—" He stopped for a second as though it hurt him even to think about his father. "He taught me a lot about woodcraft. But Jonesy wouldn't let me get any job at all. I think he was afraid if I proved I could support myself, I'd run away. So he made me work on his truck farm without pay."

"Boy, he *is* a Simon Legree," Trixie breathed excitedly.

Jim nodded in agreement. "We had a heck of an argument when school closed, and day before yesterday, I guess that was Wednesday, I decided to try to find Uncle James and see if he'd help me. I hitchhiked part of the way and walked the rest, sleeping in the woods, because I didn't have any money, you know. I wasn't sure exactly where my uncle lived, and I didn't dare ask anybody, but by luck, this morning, as I was walking along the road, I noticed the faded letters on the mailbox at the foot of the driveway. I remembered that Mother had said his place was called Ten Acres, so I came up here." He grinned. "I tell you, I was pretty disappointed when nobody answered my knock, and I saw how run-down the place was. But I was so tired I climbed in through the window and flopped down on this old mattress. So, here I am."

"Golly," Trixie gasped. "Haven't you had anything to eat since Wednesday?"

He shook his head. "A few berries I found, that's all."

Honey scrambled to her feet. "We'll go right home now and get you something. You must be starving."

"I could do with a little something," he confessed, patting his stomach. "I planned to shoot a rabbit and roast it on an outdoor spit; but, now that you mention it, I'm so hungry I doubt if I could wait long enough to skin and clean it."

"I'll be right back," Trixie declared, starting for the window. "My house is just down in the hollow over there."

"Hold on," Jim called out. "How're you going to get food out of the house without someone getting suspicious?"

"Oh, oh," Trixie admitted. "I never thought about that."

"I know," Honey broke in, "I'll tell Miss Trask we

want to have a picnic in the woods. The cook'll pack up enough food for a regiment, and we can bring it up here and have our lunch with Jim."

"Wonderful!" Trixie reached into a back pocket and produced a crushed, half-melted candy bar. "Will this keep you going till then, Jim?" she asked, offering the candy.

Jim wolfed down the chocolate and unashamedly licked the paper clean. "Thanks," he began and then stopped as the neigh of a frightened horse broke the stillness of the outside air. The three of them rushed to the open window, and, over the top of the hedge, they could see Lady and Strawberry rearing and plunging in fright.

Something was crashing wildly in the underbrush, something that was apparently caught in the tangled vines of the thicket. Jim turned back swiftly for the gun and vaulted through the window. Trixie hesitated a moment, then followed. Just as she got near the hedge, whatever it was broke free and dashed away through the woods.

"What was it?" Trixie panted as she reached Jim's side. "Did you see it?"

Jim had raised the shotgun to his shoulder and was sighting along the barrel. "It was a dog," he said as he slowly lowered the gun. "Wish I could have shot it."

"Shot it?" Trixie was aghast. "You wouldn't shoot a poor helpless dog, Jim Frayne, just because it frightened the horses?"

Jim shook his head. "It looked like a mad dog to me," he said soberly. "I'm almost sure I saw foam dripping from its muzzle."

Just then a child screamed from the depths of the woods. The helpless scream came again, and Trixie heard her name called in a high-pitched, terrified voice.

She felt her knees buckle under her. "It's Bobby," she gasped. "Bobby, alone in the woods with a mad dog!"

Chapter 4
The Brass Key

Somehow Trixie's trembling legs carried her through the thicket. She raced along the bridle path, tripping and stumbling and shouting, "Bobby, Bobby!" at the top of her lungs. And then she saw him, and as relief flooded over her, rage took its place, for Bobby was sitting calmly under a tree, grinning from ear to ear.

"Bobby Belden!" she gasped. "What do you mean by screaming like that when nothing's wrong with you?"

He tossed his silky curls. "I couldn't find you, and I want to 'splore, too. So I screamed. I knew you'd come if I screamed."

Trixie put out her arms to shake him, but then, because she really was so glad he was safe, she pulled him to her instead and hugged him tightly. "You're a bad boy, Bobby," she scolded. "Did you run away from Miss Trask?"

Bobby laid his cheek against hers, all innocence. "No, I got hungry, so I told her I had to go home for lunch. I did go home, too, but Mummy said it wasn't quite ready; so I came up here, 'cause I saw the horses.

But then when I got here, I couldn't see the horses any more." His blue eyes clouded, and Trixie realized with a tug at her heartstrings that the little boy really had been frightened. "I guess I got sort of losted," he admitted, "and I was so tired, after climbing up the hill, I just sat down and screamed." He grinned suddenly. "Hey, who was that running behind you, and why did he sneak away when he saw me?"

Then Trixie knew that Jim must have followed her, but, seeing that Bobby was safe, he had slipped away. Bobby, she decided, must never guess Jim's secret, because Bobby could never keep any secret at all. "It must have been Honey," she said quickly. "She went to get the horses, I guess."

At that moment, Honey appeared, riding Strawberry and leading Lady. "You don't have to come back to the stable with me, Trixie," she said. "Ji—"

Trixie held up a warning finger. Honey flushed. "I hear that if a dog is mad, it always runs across country in a straight line," she finished. "So we don't have to worry about its coming back."

"Well, that's good." Trixie took Bobby by the hand. "You've got to go home for your lunch now," she told him firmly. "See you later, Honey."

For once Bobby was too tired and hungry to argue.

Obediently, he let Trixie take him home and trotted right upstairs to wash his face and hands.

"I've been invited to a picnic lunch by Honey Wheeler," Trixie told her mother. "May I go if I come back afterward and take care of Bobby when he wakes up from his nap?"

"All right," Mrs. Belden agreed. "I'm glad you've found a new friend. Bobby said you went riding through the woods. Your shirt looks as though you'd had a spill. Did you?"

Trixie nodded, grinning. "It's not as easy as I thought it would be, Moms, but Regan—that's the man who takes care of the Wheelers' horses—said he'd give me lessons. He also said he was sure I'd learn fast."

"I'm sure you will, too," Mrs. Belden smiled. "But try not to break any bones in the process."

Trixie raced up the hill through the wooded path that led up from the vegetable garden to the Wheeler estate. She met Honey coming around the lake from the opposite direction. She was carrying a large, napkin-covered basket.

"I've got a whole roasted chicken and a quart of milk," she called out, "and a dozen buttered rolls, besides a lemon meringue pie." She giggled. "I told Miss Trask you had an enormous appetite."

"I have." Trixie took one handle of the basket and peeked under the snowy white napkin. "Boy, Jim'll be glad to see all this, won't he?"

As the girls entered the woods, Honey moved closer to Trixie. "Ooh," she murmured, "it's much more scary walking through here than it is riding." The trail was thickly carpeted with pine needles, and the heavy branches of the trees shaded them from the hot noon sun. Honey jumped as a chipmunk appeared from nowhere and scurried across the path. "Regan told me there were foxes and skunks in these woods," she said with a little shiver. "Do you think one of them will attack us, Trixie?"

"Golly, she is nervous," Trixie thought and said out loud, "Of course they won't, silly. Wild animals never attack humans unless we attack them first."

"How about that game hen?" Honey demanded, with a nervous laugh.

"That was different," Trixie told her. "She thought we were after her eggs." She sniffed the air. "I smell a skunk right now. Or a fox. Oh," she finished as they came around a bend in the trail, "there's a skunk, now. Isn't he cute?"

The little black and white animal stood smugly in the middle of the path, several yards ahead of them.

"Cute?" Honey cringed. "It's a horrible, smelly creature, and it'll squirt that awful stuff all over us."

"Skunks aren't really smelly at all," Trixie told her. "They're very clean little animals, and the Indians in Canada think skunk meat is delicious to eat. Mart had a pet skunk once till Dad discovered it in the chicken coop calmly eating the eggs." She laughed. "They carry that fluid in two little sacs under their tails, and when they jump around that's the time to run. Reddy didn't run fast enough once, and it was days before Mother'd let him inside the house."

"Oh, Trixie, please let's go back," Honey begged. "I'm more afraid of skunks than anything else in the woods."

"Well," Trixie said, "we're perfectly safe unless we come too close. I'm going to throw this stone at him and see if that won't make him move."

Honey let the basket slip to the ground and got ready to run. The skunk, completely ignoring the pebble that bounced beside it, unconcernedly rooted through the leaves for a bug. The second stone landed on its back. The little animal stood perfectly still as though considering the matter carefully, then after a moment, ambled slowly across the path and into the woods.

"See?" Trixie demanded triumphantly.

"Yes," Honey said doubtfully. "But did you ever hear of a mad skunk?"

"Of course not," Trixie cried in derision. "Where did you ever get such a dopey idea?"

"From Jim," Honey told her in a low voice. "He said he hoped that the dog who frightened the horses this morning didn't have rabies. He said that a mad dog will attack anything in its way, and if it bit a fox or a weasel or a skunk that animal would go mad, too, and attack anything or anybody."

"I don't believe it," Trixie said. "And, anyway, we're not sure the dog did have rabies. It could have been foaming from the mouth because it got so hot thrashing around in the tangled vines." Trixie had already forgotten how terrified she had been earlier when she thought Bobby was alone in the woods with a mad dog and was convinced that Jim had deliberately made up a story about mad animals and dogs especially, just to tease Honey.

When they arrived at the hedge, Honey drew back timidly. "You go first," she said. "I'm so jittery I think I'd faint if Queenie even cackled at me."

Trixie laughed and led the way through the thicket, calling out to let Jim know that he didn't have to hide. He promptly appeared at the window and eyed the lunch basket hungrily. "We ought to have a special signal," he said as they handed him the basket and climbed through the window. "I'll teach you how to imitate a bobwhite; then, whenever I hear that bird call, I'll always know it's you."

By the time they had spread out the picnic on the old mattress, both girls had learned how to whistle, "Bob *White!*" almost as well as Jim did.

"We really ought to clean up this place," Honey said, looking around the cluttered living-room with distaste. "You can't live here like this, Jim. It's perfectly horrible."

Jim shrugged. "It is pretty dirty, but, after all, Uncle James must have liked it this way so we have no right to change anything without his permission." He munched thoughtfully on a drumstick. "I wonder if he'll ever get well. If he doesn't, I'm out of luck."

"Dad is sure to stop by the hospital on the way home," Trixie said, making a thick sandwich out of a buttered roll and a large slab of white meat. "I'll bring you the latest news tomorrow morning."

When they finished lunch, Trixie said excitedly, "I think we ought to start right now searching for the hidden treasure. If Mr. Frayne dies without ever regaining consciousness, nobody'll ever know where it is."

"How do you know there is any hidden treasure, Trixie?" Jim teased. "There's a whole barrelful of bottle tops in the study, if that's what you mean."

Trixie ignored him. "I just have a feeling there's a ton of money or jewels or something hidden around here. Let's start looking." She scrambled to her feet.

"I wouldn't know where to begin," Honey said doubtfully.

"Neither would I," Jim agreed. "Although I suppose that big roll-top desk is the most logical place."

"I don't think we'll find it in a logical place," Trixie said. "If I were a miser and was afraid of robbers, I'd hide my treasure in the same room where I slept and in the most illogical place imaginable."

"For instance?" Jim arched his eyebrows unbelievingly.

"For instance," Trixie retorted, "this pile of old newspapers. No burglar would have the time or the patience to sort through them all but between the pages would be a swell place to hide a will or stock certificates or even money."

"You mean there might have been a method in my uncle's madness?" Jim said, thoughtfully staring at the debris.

"I wouldn't go through that pile of filthy papers for

anything," Honey said firmly. "It's probably crawling with roaches. I agree with Jim. The desk is the place to look."

But Trixie had already started riffling through the yellow sheets of faded newsprint. Jim and Honey watched her for a moment and then went into the study to search the desk. After a while, they called out that the desk was locked and that the chest of drawers contained nothing but a few acorns apparently left there by squirrels.

Jim refused to break the lock of the desk without his uncle's permission. "I keep thinking those bottle tops may be worth something," he said deridingly as they joined Trixie in the living-room. Trixie worked on and on, and pretty soon they caught some of her enthusiasm and set to work on the other two stacks which contained old magazines and pamphlets.

Trixie was nearing the bottom of her pile, and she was hot and dusty and discouraged. She was about to admit that she had been wrong when she came across a thick Sunday edition which was more neatly folded than any of the others. The newspaper was so old that it tore apart at the creases when she tried to unfold it, and a large, green-tinged brass key fell out at her feet.

"Oh, joy!" she cried triumphantly, "I'll bet this fits a treasure chest. Now all we have to do is find the chest."

Jim examined the key carefully. "It looks more like an old-fashioned door key to me," he said. "But I can't imagine why Uncle James hid it under that pile of papers."

They tried the front, back, and side doors unsuccessfully, and in the end Jim dropped the key into his silver mug. "It may fit a closet or something in one of the upstairs rooms," he said. "But we can't go up there. The staircase is boarded up, you know."

"We could climb in through one of the windows," Trixie interrupted, but Jim shook his head.

"I don't like to do that," he said soberly. "This is my uncle's home, not mine. He must have boarded up the top floors for some good reason of his own."

They were all staring up at the ceiling wondering what could be up there and why Mr. Frayne wanted it kept a secret, when they heard the sound of something moving rapidly across the floor over their heads.

Honey gave a little scream and clutched Jim's arm. "I've thought all along this house was haunted," she whispered nervously.

Even Trixie felt creepy for a moment and then she joined in Jim's laughter. "Squirrels, of course," Jim said. "Or field mice."

"Oh, Jim," Trixie said, "I'd like to explore up there."

"Well, I wouldn't," Honey said emphatically. "At this point I'd rather see a ghost than a mad squirrel."

"Silly!" Trixie hooted. "What's the idea, Jim, of scaring Honey half to death with crazy stories of mad animals?"

"They're not crazy," Jim said seriously. "I saw a mad weasel once, and I'll never forget it. I was fishing at a pond in the woods, and it came straight at me, running like fury. Lucky for me, I had hip-length rubber boots on, or I probably wouldn't be here to tell the tale. I killed it with a rock and saved the body to show to Dad, who was a naturalist, you know. He said the weasel had hydrophobia. There was a mad dog scare around the countryside that August and Dad said an infected dog had probably bitten the weasel."

Trixie sniffed. "I never heard of such a thing," she declared. "I'll bet you made the whole thing up."

Jim's face flushed with anger, and he stared at her through narrowed green eyes. "There's one thing you'd better find out right now, Trixie Belden," he said evenly. "I never make things up. That was one of the reasons why I left Jonesy. He didn't believe me when I told him I'd won a scholarship to college. I didn't bother to show him the letter from the principal of my high school. I just left." And without another word he stalked across the room and vaulted out of the window.

Trixie felt hot and cold with shame. She knew she had the habit of hurting people's feelings sometimes, without meaning to. Her mother and father and even her older brothers had often told her she should count to ten before jumping to conclusions, but she never seemed to remember in time. Hot tears burned back of her eyes, and she had to swallow hard before she could call out, "I'm sorry, Jim. I didn't mean it."

There was no answer, and Honey said quietly, "Don't feel so badly, Trixie. Jim's a very sensitive boy, but he thinks a lot of you. He told me so this morning when he came back after making sure that Bobby was all right. He said it took an awful lot of courage for you to run through the woods right after a mad dog had been there." Shyly she tucked Trixie's arm through hers. "I wish I wasn't such a fraidy cat. I sat there on the window sill so scared I couldn't move and watched you two tearing through the brambles and wondered what it would be like not to be afraid all the time."

Trixie swallowed again and felt better. "Are you really afraid all the time, Honey? Honest?"

Honey nodded. "Yes, and especially at night. I have awful nightmares sometimes, and when I was sick, I had nightmares all the time. I keep dreaming over and over that I'm in a tiny little sealed room, and a great big heavy balloon is pressing down on me. It keeps pressing down until I can't breathe, and then I wake up screaming."

Trixie squeezed her arm sympathetically. "Gosh, it must be awful. I haven't had any nightmares since I was a kid."

"It is awful," Honey said. "Miss Trask says it's just nerves, and when I start eating better I'll get over it."

"Start eating better?" Trixie stared at her in amazement. "Why you ate as much as Jim and I did at lunch today. We all ate like pigs!"

Honey flushed with embarrassment, and she bent down to hide her face as she folded the napkin back into the empty basket. "I know I did, Trixie," she said, "but I was hungry today for the first time in my life. I guess," she added quietly, "that was because today was the first time, too, that I ever remember having had any fun." She straightened suddenly. "I'm glad now that my family moved up here. If they hadn't, why, g-gosh, I might never have met you and Jim!"

Chapter 5
Copperhead!

When Trixie got home, she found her mother dressed for her Garden Club meeting in the village.

"I'm leaving Bobby in your care," she said as she slid behind the wheel of the station wagon. "You might keep him with you while you do some weeding. Don't forget to gather the eggs and throw out a canful of scratch for the chickens around five o'clock. Your father filled the mash hoppers this morning, but you had better check the water." She turned on the ignition. "I did the luncheon dishes and the dusting and made a big pitcher of lemonade. There are plenty of cookies in the crock. I thought you might like to have your new friend to tea."

"Oh, Moms!" Trixie jumped on the running board and kissed her mother swiftly. "You're just wonderful. You think of everything." Thoughtfully, she watched the station wagon roll down the driveway under the arch of crabapple trees. "I'm the lucky duck, not Honey," she told herself. "I have what she calls fun all the time. From now on, I'm going to work like a beaver to show Dad and

Moms how glad I am I belong to them and not to Honey's father and mother."

Bobby began to wail then, as he always did when he woke up from his nap. Trixie raced upstairs and found him sprawled across his bunk, sleepily rubbing his eyes. "I'm too hot," he howled. "And I won't wear oberalls. I wanna wear my bathing suit, and you squirt me with the hose."

"I'll squirt you, later," Trixie said soothingly. "Come on, Bobby, I'll help you with your overall straps and sandals."

"Don't wanna wear sandals," he said crossly, squirming away from her. "Wanna go barefoot."

"All right," Trixie agreed, "but you've got to stay right with me in the garden, then. You can help me weed, and then, afterward, we can have lemonade and cookies out on the terrace."

Bobby cheered up immediately. "I can weed, too," he announced as they walked across the lawn to the garden path. "Mummy showed me this morning which little plants were lamb's quarters and which ones were carrots." He grinned. "I picked an awful lot of carrots first before she 'splained to me."

"You can pull up the purslane," Trixie told him. "They're easy to pick and good to eat. Better than lettuce."

"I won't eat 'em," Bobby said firmly. "'Member the time I ate poison ivy?"

Trixie shuddered. Bobby had heard his older brothers saying that the Indians obtained immunity from poison ivy and poison sumac by chewing the leaves. He had been a very sick little boy for several days. "No, you'd better not eat anything," Trixie cautioned.

" 'Cept lemonade and cookies," Bobby said as he raced ahead of her and tripped over the patch of exposed tree roots.

"Oh, Bobby," Trixie cried impatiently. "Must you trip over roots every single time?"

He scrambled to his feet and picked up his trowel and pail. "Not every single time," he said with injured pride. "Once I tripped over a big black snake, right here. He was so long," he said stretching out his arms full length. "And he didn't bite me, or anything."

"Of course, he didn't bite you," Trixie said. "Snakes don't go around biting people." She hustled the little boy into the fenced-in garden and closed the gate just in time to keep out Reddy who liked nothing better than to run up and down the neat green rows in pursuit of an imaginary rabbit. Reddy sat outside the gate for a while and looked sulkily after them. Then he grew tired of waiting and set off after a squirrel.

Bobby promptly sat down on a carefully tied-up head of lettuce and announced that he was going to dig for worms instead of weeding. "You're worse than Reddy," Trixie scolded him as she moved him to the path. "Now, stay right there and don't dig up anything except this purslane."

Trixie noticed, then, that the tomato seedlings her mother had transplanted that morning were drooping sadly in the hot sun. These plants would bear a late crop of green tomatoes which her mother would pick just before the first frost, and they would ripen slowly indoors so the family could have fresh tomatoes up until Christmas. "I'd better water them after I feed the chickens," Trixie said. "Otherwise, they're sure to die."

She worked along the row of broccoli plants, weeding and cultivating with her scratcher but thinking mostly about Jim and Honey. *I hope Jim isn't still mad at me,* she thought with a little pang of regret. *I'll apologize the first thing in the morning.* She began to wonder, then, whether old Mr. Frayne would ever get well and whether or not there really was hidden wealth up at the old Mansion. She was lost in thought when she was startled out of her preoccupation by Bobby's screams.

She scrambled stiffly up from her knees, momentarily blinded by the bright sunlight shining in her eyes. Then she saw that the gate was open and there was no sign of Bobby.

"Trixie!" he screamed again, and she realized that he was somewhere in the woods just outside the garden. For a moment panic seized her; Bobby's screams usually meant that he was in trouble, for Bobby was almost always in some sort of trouble. But then she remembered how he had screamed earlier that day just to attract her attention, and she called out sharply, "What *is* the matter, Bobby? Where *are* you?"

"I'm here," he called, and she saw him, then, at the edge of the woods waving a forked stick. "I caught a snake," he said, half-crying, half-laughing. "But he didn't like it, and you were wrong. He did bite me." He stuck out his bare foot as she ran to him. "He bitted me on the toe. It burns."

Panic swept back over Trixie as she saw the drops of blood on Bobby's big toe. *It could have been a copperhead,* she thought wildly. *Oh, no, no. It must have been a black snake. They get very bold when they're teased.* Aloud she asked in as calm a voice as she could muster, "What did it look like, Bobby? Was it a black snake? Tell me quickly, was it long and black?"

Without even waiting for his answer, she made a

hasty tourniquet with her handkerchief and a stick and twisted it tightly around the bleeding toe.

Bobby's lower lip began to tremble as he sensed her panic. "It wasn't black," he sobbed. "It was sort of brown with spots and stripes. Ooh, that's too tight. It hurts."

But Trixie had already scooped him up into her arms and was running back to the house as fast as she could. "It was probably nothing but a harmless little garter snake," she kept telling herself to keep her legs from buckling under her. "But it might have been a copperhead. Oh, why did I let him go barefoot?" she reproached herself. "Why didn't I keep him in the garden with me?"

She laid him gently on the living-room sofa and ran upstairs, calling, "Lie perfectly still, Bobby. Everything's going to be all right. Just lie still." In her father's medicine cabinet, she found a new razor blade wrapped in sterile paper. Just then, she heard someone calling her name, and, looking out the window, she saw Honey coming up the driveway.

Trixie leaned out the bathroom window, whispering hoarsely, "Bobby was bitten by a snake. I don't want to frighten him, and I don't know whether it was a copperhead or not, but I've got to give him first aid, anyway, because we might not be able to get a doctor out here from town for half an hour."

She tore downstairs and almost collided with Honey in the hall. "You hold him in your arms," she whispered to Honey, "while I cut the fang marks with this razor blade. The quieter he is, the less chance there'll be of the poison spreading."

Luckily, Bud had followed Honey into the house, and Bobby was so happy hugging the little puppy he hardly felt the quick incisions Trixie made in his toe. "I'm going to suck out as much blood as I can with my mouth," Trixie told Honey over her shoulder. "You call Doctor Ferris and ask him to come out right away with the antivenin. The phone's in the study, and the doctor's number's on a card on the wall over the desk."

When Honey came back saying that Dr. Ferris was on his way, Bobby was laughing. "Trixie's pretending to be a mosquito," he said. "She's sucking all the blood out of my toe."

With half of her consciousness, between sucking and spitting out the blood and venom, Trixie noticed that Honey's face was as white as a sheet and wondered vaguely if she herself looked as sick.

"That tourniquet must have been on fifteen minutes, now," she told herself after a while. "I'll have to take it off for a minute." Gratefully she saw that the swelling in Bobby's toe had not yet spread to his foot, so she replaced the tourniquet where she had put it originally, sucking and spitting all the time. Every now and then Bobby complained that his toe felt like it was on fire, so Trixie knew there could be no doubt, now, that he had been bitten by a copperhead.

It seemed like hours before they heard the crunch of tires on the gravel driveway, and every minute of the long wait Trixie lived in her imagination with old Mr. Frayne and his wife on that lonely road in a car that wouldn't start. "I guess I'd go crazy, too, if that happened to me," she admitted, almost hysterically. "Oh, Bobby, Bobby, you've just got to get well!"

Dr. Ferris came quickly into the room and crossed over to where Trixie was kneeling beside the little boy. "How long has this tourniquet been on?" he asked as he carefully examined the bleeding, swollen toe.

"About fifteen minutes for the second time," Trixie said anxiously, as she glanced at the clock over the fireplace.

Dr. Ferris opened his black leather case. "Then you've applied suction for half an hour?" As Trixie nodded, he removed the tourniquet and took out his hypodermic syringe. "Then that's all we need of that," he said quietly. "Now, I want to wrap this boy in a blanket and pack the toe in ice. Then we'll give him some nice hot tea, just in case he has suffered any shock."

Trixie had to clench her teeth to keep them from chattering as she got the blanket and ice and put water on to boil. She left Honey in the kitchen making the tea and when she came back into the living-room, the doctor was repacking his kit. He smiled at her reassuringly.

"You did a good job, Trixie," he said, "so I only gave him a little of the antivenin. Lucky I had a fresh supply on hand. Ordered some last week in case those boys at that camp up the river got into trouble."

"Doctor Ferris gave me a shot," Bobby told Trixie with a weak little grin. "And I didn't yell. I *never* yell when I get a shot."

Trixie swallowed hard. "You're a very brave boy, Bobby," she said softly. "Very, *very* brave." Trixie's knees were shaking now.

Honey came in with the tray then, and her hands were shaking so that the cup and saucer rattled against each other. When Bobby had finished drinking the hot tea through a straw the kindly old doctor lifted him gently and carried him carefully upstairs to his bed. "We'll have to keep you quiet for a few days, young man," he said, "and then you'll be as good as new." He tucked blankets around the little boy and turned to Trixie. "Just let me examine your mouth, Trixie," he said, producing a little flashlight from his pocket. "Ah, good, good. There aren't any cuts or sores."

Trixie heard the station wagon in the driveway then, and she ran out to tell her mother what had happened. Mrs. Belden's face was pale as Honey's as she hurried past Trixie into the house and up the stairs. Dr. Ferris was assuring her that there was nothing to worry about when Trixie followed her mother into Bobby's room. Trixie's legs were shaking again, and she had to bite her lips to keep back the tears. "It was all my fault," she kept telling herself. "All my fault."

"Trixie worked so quickly with the tourniquet and the cut and suck method," Dr. Ferris was saying cheerfully, "that I doubt if Bobby really needed the antivenin. He may suffer from shock, so keep him warm and quiet. He'll probably run quite a high fever tonight, but don't worry. He's a husky lad and he couldn't have been bitten in a safer place, if it had to happen." He laid his hand on Trixie's shoulder. "You're a very level-headed young lady," he said. "Any time you decide you want a job as a nurse just let me know."

"Thank you, Trixie," Mrs. Belden said, her face

buried in Bobby's neck. "Your father is going to be very proud of you."

Trixie felt sickeningly weak, then, and her whole body began to shake. If her mother had scolded her for not taking better care of Bobby, she would have felt better. Choking sobs welled up in her throat, and she turned and ran blindly out of the room and into the hall.

Downstairs, she flung herself on the sofa and let the tears come. From somewhere far off, she heard Honey say, "I guess I'll be going home now, Trixie. That is, unless I can help you in some way."

Trixie got out a mumbled, "Thanks for everything, Honey," and lay there crying quietly until she heard her father come in the door.

Chapter 6
A Runaway

Trixie slept late the next morning. She had hardly closed her eyes all night, worrying about Bobby and listening to her father and mother as they took turns sitting with him. When she woke up, the first thing she did was to tiptoe to his room to see how he was.

Mrs. Belden smiled at her from the rocking chair beside Bobby's bunk. "He's fine, Trixie," she said. "He had very little fever last night, and there's almost no swelling in his foot. Doctor Ferris stopped by early this morning and said he's out of all danger, now. We won't have to worry about him."

Bobby looked feverish, and there were dark lines under his eyes. "Go 'way," he told Trixie in a weak, fretful voice. "Mummy's reading to me."

"You stay with him, Moms," Trixie cried impulsively. "I'll take care of the house and the chickens and everything."

"Dad cooked breakfast," Mrs. Belden said, with a laugh. "A whole pound of bacon, I gather, and I imagine he left the dishes for you. But he's bringing a practical nurse out from the village to help me, and he said explicitly that he wanted you to go ahead and have your riding lesson." Trixie flushed, remembering how her father had praised her the evening before. "Just give the downstairs a lick and a promise," her mother finished, "and then run along. Honey is here. She has been waiting for you since nine."

Trixie found Honey in the bright red and white kitchen. "I arrived just as the doctor was leaving," she told Trixie. "I was awfully glad to hear that Bobby's going to be all right." She pirouetted around the room. "How do you like my dungarees? Miss Trask drove to White Plains for them yesterday afternoon."

"Great!" Trixie gulped down a big glass of cold orange juice and spread butter on slices of bread for a bacon sandwich. "I'd better make several of these," she said. "You-know-who is probably ravenous this morning."

Honey shook her head. "No, he's all taken care of. I went up there when your mother said you were still asleep. I smuggled some dry cereal and hard-boiled eggs out of our kitchen, but he'd already eaten. At least, he was just starting. He'd shot a rabbit and was cooking it over an outdoor spit. He gave me a piece; and, Trixie, I never tasted anything so delicious."

Trixie grinned. "You and your birdlike appetite!"

"I'm hungry all the time now," Honey admitted, smiling. "I had eggs and cereal for breakfast, rabbit with Jim, and that bacon smelled so good I had a sandwich while I was waiting for you." She sobered suddenly. "But I had an awful dream last night. The worst nightmare I ever had. I'll tell you about it on the way over to our place. Regan's waiting to give you a lesson in posting."

"Tell me, now," Trixie said, bringing her dishes to the piled-up sink. "I've got to do some straightening-up around here before I can leave for the stables with you."

"I'll dry." Honey slipped a dish towel off the rack. "I learned to do dishes and make beds at camp, so I'll help."

"Wonderful," Trixie cried enthusiastically. And, with Honey's assistance, it took them less than half an hour to tidy up the house. While they swept and dusted, Honey related her dream.

"I was walking through the woods," she said, with a reminiscent shiver. "It was so real I still can't believe I was only dreaming. Anyway, I was walking along toward the Miser's Mansion and it was all quiet and creepy the way it is in the thick part of the woods, when suddenly I heard something rustling along the path ahead of me. It was a great big black snake with a thick white stripe down its back, and it was coming toward

me as fast as it could. I just stood there, too scared to move or scream or anything. You know how it is in dreams—you're just rooted to the spot."

Trixie nodded sympathetically. "And then what?"

"And then, just as it reached my feet, I woke up," Honey continued. "I was dripping wet with cold perspiration, and I guess I must have cried out without knowing it, because Miss Trask was bending over me, wiping my face with a damp washcloth and speaking softly."

Trixie wondered why it was always Miss Trask, and never Honey's mother, who came when Honey was frightened, but she said nothing.

"I told her about the dream," Honey went on, "and she said it was perfectly natural for me to have a nightmare like that after what happened to Bobby, yesterday. I'm surprised you didn't have a nightmare yourself, Trixie."

"The whole thing was a nightmare to me," Trixie said, "and I was so upset I couldn't sleep long enough to have a bad dream."

"You didn't seem upset at all," Honey cried admiringly. "You were perfectly wonderful. I don't know how you did all the right things without losing your head."

They cut across the lawn to the path that led to the Wheeler estate, and Honey said, "Oh, I meant to tell you the first thing. Jim isn't mad at you any more. He said he was sorry he lost his temper yesterday, and when I told him about my dream, he said you were right. He shouldn't have frightened me with stories about mad animals, because the chances of my being attacked by one are about one in a million." She flushed. "I told him I was scared of everything, anyway, so he hadn't really made things any worse."

"Well, I shouldn't have accused him of lying," Trixie said quickly. "And I'm glad he's not mad. I like Jim and I feel awfully sorry for him. If you ask me, I think he's jumped out of the frying pan into the fire by running away. I can't believe his stepfather could be any meaner to him than old man Frayne would be."

"I don't know about that," Honey said as she walked along the narrow path behind Trixie. "Jim's terribly afraid of Jonesy. What worries me is that his stepfather may be looking for him right now, and why wouldn't the Mansion be the most obvious place?"

"That's right," Trixie agreed. "It'd be horrible if Jonesy should sneak up there at night and catch Jim in his sleep. But what worries *me* is that even if his uncle does get well, he may not be any nicer to Jim than Jonesy was. Oh, ginger," she interrupted herself, "that reminds me. I forgot to ask Dad last night how Mr. Frayne was."

"I figured you'd forget in all the excitement," Honey said, "so I called the hospital the first chance I got this morning, saying I was a neighbor. The nurse who answered the phone wouldn't say anything except that the patient's condition was unchanged. I guess that means he's still unconscious, doesn't it?"

"I guess so," Trixie said. "I hope he doesn't die without telling somebody where he hid his money."

"I wish I was as sure as you are," Honey said doubtfully, "that there is some money. It must be terrible to be poor and not have a father or mother or anybody to care about you."

Regan was exercising Jupiter when they arrived at the stable and had Lady and Strawberry saddled and bridled, waiting for them. "Up you go," he told Trixie cheerfully. "And, unless I don't know a natural-born rider when I see one, you'll learn how to post a trot this very morning."

Regan's prediction turned out to be true. Although Trixie was jostled about a lot the first few minutes and almost lost her stirrups again, she found to her delight at the end of the lesson that she could grip with her knees and rise up to meet Lady's gait almost as rhythmically as Honey. She was trotting around the field with Regan beside her on Jupiter when he was called into the

house to answer the phone. Regan dismounted and handed Honey Jupiter's reins. "You two just walk the horses till I get back," he said.

"Boy," Trixie cried when Regan had gone, "I'm dying to ride Jupiter, Honey. Couldn't I just walk him around the field once while you lead Lady, instead?"

"I wouldn't," Honey said cautiously. "He's got an awfully strong mouth, Trixie, and Regan's only got a snaffle bit on him today. If he started to run, you'd never be able to stop him. Even Dad won't ride him outside of the corral without a curb bit."

"Pooh." Trixie slipped out of her saddle. "He's as gentle as a lamb, and I won't let him out of a walk. I just want to know how it feels to be on the back of such a beautiful creature as Jupiter."

"Well, I guess you'll be all right." Honey reluctantly transferred the reins. "But I'd feel safer if they'd finished fencing in this field."

While Trixie was mounting, Jupiter stood perfectly still, but the minute she was in the saddle he tossed his head, and, as she was bending forward slightly, he hit her hard in the face. Blinded with tears of pain, Trixie gathered up the reins too quickly, and Jupiter stepped right out into a fast trot. Trixie jerked at the leather, trying to pull him down to a walk, and Jupiter broke into a canter. Too late, Trixie realized that she had about as much hope of controlling this horse as she would a steam engine. Faster and faster, he raced around the field, and as Honey, shouting, "Whoa, Jupe, Whoa!" tried to cut him off, he swerved sharply and galloped out of the corral and up the path to the woods near the old Mansion.

The stirrups, which had been adjusted to Regan's long legs, swung free, but the big horse's gallop was so smooth Trixie managed to keep her seat by leaning forward slightly and gripping his sides tightly with her legs and knees. Branches whipped against her face, and a spray of pebbles flew out from under the horse's feet. Trixie was so frightened she couldn't do anything but hang on and wonder what was going to happen when the trail ended at the hedge around Miser's Mansion. Would Jupiter turn there and take the downtrail to the hollow and Crabapple Farm?

Trixie knew she wasn't a good enough rider to stay on the horse's back if he ran downhill. *I'll be thrown over his head,* she thought hopelessly, *and he won't be able to stop, so I'll be trampled under his feet.*

They flew around a bend in the trail, and there, smack in front of them, was the almost impenetrable hedge. For one awful second, Trixie was sure Jupiter planned to plunge right through the thick underbrush, but at that moment the game cock, on the other side of the hedge, suddenly flapped its wings and burst into a loud, triumphant crow. Jupiter shied in astonishment, planted his forefeet, and stopped dead in his tracks.

Trixie shot over his head as though she had been jet-propelled and landed in the bushes. Although she was dazed by the fall, she saw Jim slip silently from the hedge and grab Jupiter's dangling reins. The big black horse reared once and came down dangerously close to where Trixie was sprawling, then quieted to a nervous standstill.

"There, boy," Jim was saying soothingly, "it's all right, boy. Nobody's going to hurt you." And, without changing the tone of his voice, he added to Trixie, "You're a little fool to let a horse run like that on such a hot day." He patted Jupiter's sweat-soaked neck. "There, boy."

"*Let* him?" Trixie scrambled to her feet, rubbing a bruised hip. "He let me stay on his back, but that's about all I had to do with it," she said sourly.

Jim grinned. "I heard a horse pounding along the path, and it sounded like a runaway to me, so I slipped into the bushes to watch. I figured that, even if it wasn't a runaway, whoever was riding the horse was going to have a nasty spill when the horse took the downhill fork." Jupiter nuzzled Jim's shirt. "Gee, I'd like to ride this fellow," Jim said. "Is he yours, Trixie?"

Trixie shook her head. "No, he belongs to Honey's father. I had no business getting on his back at all. I'm just learning to ride, you see; but he's so beautiful I couldn't resist it."

"I don't blame you," Jim said as he handed Trixie the reins. "Someone's coming along the trail on horseback now. Sounds like two horses. I'll duck into the house. Whistle when it's safe for me to come out."

It was Regan on Strawberry, and in a minute Honey appeared on Lady. Regan looked very cross and red in the face. He paid no attention to Trixie, except to snatch Jupiter's bridle from her, and went back down the trail without a word.

"I've spoiled everything," Trixie wailed. "He's furious, and he'll never give me any more riding lessons."

Honey slid off Lady's back. "Don't worry about Regan, Trixie," she said comfortingly. "He gets over being mad very quickly, and I honestly think he admires you for daring to ride Jupiter. He was awfully worried when he came out of the house and saw you tearing into the woods. I was too, Trixie," she said gently. "You could have been killed."

"I guess nobody was as scared as I was," Trixie

admitted. "But when I was flying through the air over Jupe's head, all I thought of was that he might run down the hill, trip on the reins and get a bad fall." She told Honey, then, about Jim appearing just in time, and both girls whistled, "Bob *White!*" in unison.

In a minute or two, Jim came through the bushes. He patted Lady and fed her a carrot he had pulled in the garden. "I may sound like I'm boasting," he told Honey, "but I bet I could ride your father's horse. Dad had a big black gelding like that, and I could manage him when I was only five years old. I learned to ride bareback with nothing but a halter rope to guide him."

"If you're smart," Trixie said ruefully, "you'll never touch Jupe without a curb bit."

"I wouldn't," Jim said. "Not until he got used to me, anyway. Gee, do you think you could fix it so I could ride him, sometime? I haven't ridden anything but Jonesy's big old farm horses since Dad died. That's not really riding."

"I'll fix it, somehow," Honey promised impulsively. Then her hazel eyes sparkled. "I tell you how we can arrange it. Regan always has Sunday afternoons off, and Miss Trask always takes a nap after Sunday dinner. Mother and Dad are leaving tonight for Canada, so I'm pretty sure I can lead Jupe up here for you to ride tomor-row as soon as Regan leaves."

Jim's face flushed as he said, "Gosh, Honey, that would be swell. Thanks." He turned to Trixie, then. "How's your kid brother?" he asked. "Honey told me he was bitten by a copperhead."

Trixie shuddered. "I can't bear to talk about it. But he's all right now."

"It's a good thing you know your first aid," Jim said approvingly, and Trixie realized with relief that he really had forgiven her for doubting the story he had told the day before.

"Let's tie up Lady and look inside the Mansion some more for your uncle's money," she said, turning toward the big house. "I just know we're going to find something."

"That's what I did all yesterday afternoon," Jim said. "I've just about given up hope."

"Well, *I* haven't." Trixie determinedly led the way through the thicket. "And I'll bet that brass key has something to do with it."

They were halfway across the clearing when Trixie heard a dog barking down in the road below the Mansion. "It doesn't sound like Reddy or Bud," she said thoughtfully. "But there aren't any other dogs around here."

"You girls had better get inside the house," Jim interrupted quietly as the barking came nearer and they could hear the animal running up the hill. "There *is* a strange dog around here. I saw it this morning, a vicious-looking mongrel." They climbed quickly in through the window. "I don't know whether it's the same one that got tangled in the vines yesterday or not," Jim said, picking up his gun. "But I'm not taking any chances. A stray dog that's been running wild for a long time can become very ugly."

Chapter 7
A New Hiding Place

The girls crowded around Jim at the window. Suddenly, with a loud squawking, Queenie burst out of the woods and flew into the clearing. Right behind her was a thin, mean-looking cur whose yellowish coat was matted with burrs. It wore no collar, and its cruel mouth was flecked with foam. Jim raised his gun to his shoulder.

Trixie grabbed his arm. "Don't shoot," she begged. "You might miss and hit Queenie."

At that moment, the plucky little game hen turned in midair and came down, clawing and scratching, on the mongrel's nose. The dog skidded to a stop, struck out at Queenie with one paw; then, with its tail between its legs, slunk into the thicket. At the same moment Queenie, squawking as though in pain, and dragging one wing, darted across the courtyard and disappeared under a clump of thickly matted bushes.

They could hear the dog running away through the woods in the opposite direction, and Trixie cried out, "Oh, oh! It's hurt poor little Queenie. We must try to catch her and fix her wing."

She was out of the window and across the clearing in a second, tearing at the vines and branches which cut off her view of Queenie's hiding place. Then she got down on her hands and knees and began crawling after the game hen. Sharp twigs scratched her face and pulled her curly blond hair, but she struggled on.

Jim was right behind her. "Let me go first, Trixie," he argued. "Queenie may fly in your face and scratch you badly."

At that moment, Trixie tripped and plunged forward, bumping her head against something hard. She scrambled quickly to a crouching position and, with Jim's help, pulled at the overhanging boughs and vines until they could see the lower half of the door which was blocking their path.

"It's the summerhouse," Trixie cried excitedly. "We've found it at last!"

"I guess you're right," Jim said as together they tugged away at the heavy branches which covered the rest of the door. "And we're in what once must have been a little arbor leading to it."

They tried the rustic door but it was locked, and the windows on either side were so thickly covered with dirt they couldn't see inside. "The key!" Trixie suddenly shouted. "The brass key, Jim. I'll bet it fits."

But Jim was already crawling back through the arbor, and in a minute or two he reappeared, making the passageway larger so that Honey could follow him. Honey winced away from the vines and was sure every time she put her hand down on a stick it would turn into a snake, so Jim had the door open by the time she joined the others.

"I'm going in first," Jim told Trixie firmly as she started across the threshold. "I brought some matches. It'll be safer if I investigate before you girls come in."

Trixie opened her mouth to argue but even in that half-light she could see the stern, stubborn set to Jim's jaw, and waited impatiently until he called out, "Okay. Nothing but spiders and a few old squirrels' nests."

By the light of matches, they could see that the summerhouse was one long room with two large windows on each of the four sides.

"It's more like a detached sunporch than a house," Trixie said. "But I imagine it was cool out here in the evenings when they had the windows open."

Jim nodded. "And it's on a higher spot of the grounds than the main floor of the big house, so they must have had a good view of the river from here."

Honey, who was too afraid of spiders to venture far inside, said from the entrance, "I suppose your uncle let it get overgrown like this because he didn't want to have anything around to remind him of the tragedy."

"I suppose so," Jim agreed. "One thing is certain, nobody would ever have discovered it if Trixie hadn't barged right into it. Say, that gives me an idea. This'll be a swell place to hide if anyone comes snooping around here. The old latticework is so rotten and covered with vines nobody would ever guess there was once an arbor leading to the door."

"Do you think your stepfather may be looking for you now, Jim?" Honey asked.

Jim shook his head. "Not yet. I know that guy. He's telling everyone right now that I won't have the courage to stay away very long, and he's describing the licking I'm going to get when I do come cringing back." There was a note of such grim determination in Jim's voice that both girls knew that, no matter what happened, Jim would never return to Jonesy.

We've just got to find that money, Trixie thought desperately. Aloud she said, "Well, there's obviously no hidden treasure in here, and I'd better go home now and see if Mother needs me."

"I'll go with you," Honey said. "But what about that dog, Jim?" she asked timidly. "Won't he come back?"

"I don't know," Jim said as he crawled after them to

the clearing. "I got a good look at him just now, and I don't think he's got rabies. A mad dog wouldn't have slunk away like that. Anyway, Queenie proved that he really is a coward, so I don't think any of us would have any trouble scaring him away with a stick or a stone."

Honey shivered. "But there was such a mean look in his yellow eyes!"

"That look," Jim explained, "is really fear. The poor brute probably ran away from someone who treated him cruelly. It's a funny thing," he went on. "A wolf, unless it's starving and is pretty sure you're helpless, won't attack you. But a wild dog that has been ill-treated will, simply because it's afraid of being attacked first. I feel sorry for that mongrel," he added, more to himself than to the girls. "I know what it's like to run away from someone who beats you for no reason at all."

"Oh, gosh, Jim," Trixie cried impulsively, "I hope your uncle gets well and takes you away from that old Jonesy."

Jim shrugged. "It doesn't look as though he will now, but don't you worry about me. I'll get along." He grinned. "And don't bother to bring me any more food for a couple of days. I've enough to last me for quite a while." He waved good-by to them from the window as they started down the path.

"Jim is really wonderful," Honey said enthusiastically. "I'm not nearly as scared of that dog as I was. I almost feel sorry for the poor thing, myself."

"Me, too," Trixie said. "Say, would you like a bike lesson, now, if Mother doesn't need me?"

"Oh, yes," Honey cried. "I'm dying to start."

Trixie found a big, cheerful-looking woman in a stiff white uniform bustling around in the kitchen. "Your little brother's doing fine," she told Trixie, "and your mother is taking a nap. I'm fixing sandwiches and soup for lunch."

"I'll help," Trixie offered.

The nurse laid her hand on Trixie's shoulder. "No, thank you, dear. You had a dreadful experience yesterday. Run along and have some fun and try to forget all about it."

"All right," Trixie said. "I'll be out on the driveway if you need me, and please give Bobby my love."

Honey had her first bicycle lesson that morning, and after a few tumbles she got on very well.

"You're really doing swell," Trixie said, watching her pupil admiringly. "I guess all the horseback riding you've done has given you a marvelous sense of balance."

Honey flushed with pleasure. "Do you think I'm

good enough to coast down that little slope from the garage?" she asked.

"Sure." Trixie grinned. "At the rate you're going, you'll be coasting down your own driveway in no time."

Honey started at the entrance to the garage and swept past Trixie, with her light-brown hair flying behind her. "Whee," she yelled excitedly, "I never had so much fun!"

At that moment, the big laundry truck lumbered into the Belden driveway, and almost simultaneously Honey lost control of the bicycle. It began to weave from side to side, right in the path of the truck as Trixie shouted, "Steer to the right, Honey. Steer to the right!"

Honey jerked the handlebars violently to one side and crashed to the ground, helplessly tangled between the two wheels. The truck driver slammed on his brakes just in time and stopped in a swirl of gravel not two feet from where Honey lay.

"Say, what goes on here?" he demanded crossly as Trixie tried to extricate Honey. "Why'n't you look where you're going?"

Trixie ignored him as he strode past them with the bundle, muttering angrily to himself. She helped Honey to her feet. Then she saw the ugly gash on Honey's knee.

"Oh, that must hurt," she cried sympathetically.

"We'd better go in the house and bathe it and put on some iodine."

Honey giggled. "My brand new dungarees, torn to shreds." She stopped suddenly and turned deathly pale. "Oh, oh," she moaned. "It's bleeding. I'm going to faint. I can't stand the sight of blood."

Trixie remembered, then, how white Honey's face had been the day before when she saw her sucking blood from Bobby's toe. With one quick movement, she sat Honey down on the lawn and pushed her head between her knees.

"You're all right, Honey," she said quietly. "You're not going to faint. Just keep your head down. I'll be right back." And she raced to the brook to soak her handkerchief. Trixie squeezed water on Honey's wrists and bathed her forehead, and in a little while the color began to come back in Honey's face and lips.

"I feel better now," she said with a shaky little laugh. "I'm sorry to be such a sissy, Trixie."

"You're not a sissy," Trixie said staunchly. "You had an awful scare and that's a nasty cut. If you feel strong enough now, Honey, we'd better go in and give it a little first aid."

Honey set her teeth while Trixie bathed the gravel out of the wound and painted it with iodine, but she

didn't utter a sound. Mrs. Belden came into the bathroom then and inspected Honey's knee. "That's an ugly gash," she said. "You'd better stay off the bike until it heals, Honey."

"Oh, Mrs. Belden," Honey wailed. "I can't. I'm just beginning to get the idea, and I'll have to start all over again if I wait."

Mrs. Belden smiled and reached up to a box on one of the shelves. "Well," she said, "keep it bandaged and wear these knee pads for a while. You're a brave girl," she added as she left the room, "to risk bumping that knee again so soon."

Honey stared at Trixie. "Do you suppose she really meant that?" she gasped. "About my being brave? Or was she just trying to make me feel better?"

Trixie hooted. "Of course she meant it, silly. Moms never says anything she doesn't mean."

"Gosh," Honey breathed. "Golly! Golly! Golly!"

Chapter 8
An Exploring Trip

Trixie was just finishing her soup and sandwich when the phone rang. It was Honey, breathless with excitement.

"Oh, Trixie, what do you think just arrived by express?"

"A big black snake with a white streak down its back," Trixie teased, and then she could have bitten off her tongue as she realized from the silence on the other end of the wire that she had hurt Honey's feelings. She was relieved after a couple of seconds to hear a giggle.

"No, a bike," Honey said. "Miss Trask ordered it yesterday when she was in White Plains. It's a beauty, too, with a big basket and a speedometer and a siren and a lamp. I'm going to practice all afternoon, so maybe I'll be good enough by tomorrow to go for a long ride with you."

"Great," Trixie said. "I bike to the store about a mile away every Sunday morning for the New York papers. We can go right after breakfast if you think you can make it."

"Oh, wonderful," Honey cried. "Are you going up to you-know-where this afternoon?"

"No," Trixie told her. "I've got to help Mother cultivate the garden. It hasn't rained in over two weeks, you know, and the ground's as hard as a brick. We've got to loosen the dirt around the plants and then water them or they'll die."

"Can you come up for a swim later?" Honey asked.

"I'd love it." Trixie put the phone back in the cradle and went upstairs to see how Bobby was getting along.

"Hey," he greeted her in his normal voice. "Did you see that skinny old yellow dog? I saw him out of the window this morning," he went on, without waiting for her answer, "and you know what? He caught a rabbit in our rock garden and ate it all up, skin and bones and all!" He grinned.

He's really awful cute, Trixie thought giving him a quick hug. "How do you feel, Bobby?" she asked.

"I feel fine," he said cheerfully. "But last night I didn't. My foot burned all the time just like my finger did that time I forgot to spit on it first before touching the stove to make it sizzle."

Trixie laughed. "Hurry up and get well," she said. "Honey says you can have riding lessons, too, as soon as the doctor says you're well enough."

"Whoopee!" Bobby began to bounce up and down in the bed, and the nurse hurried into the room.

"Quiet! Quiet, young man," she said severely, and to Trixie, "Your mother's waiting for you in the garden. Don't you come around and excite my patient again." Then she smiled.

After hoeing for a couple of hours, Trixie thought she just had to get out of the hot sun. "I hate this old vegetable garden," she muttered crossly to herself. "I don't know why Moms is so crazy about it. But if she can stand this heat, I guess I can!"

At that moment, Mrs. Belden drew off her gloves and fanned her face with her big straw hat. "It's too hot for me, Trixie," she said, "and your face is the color of a baby beet. As soon as the sun gets lower in the sky I'll need you to help me water the plants, but between now and then you may as well get cooled off up at the lake."

Trixie dropped her hoe gratefully and raced back to the house for her bathing suit. As she hurried along the path to the Manor House, she saw Honey wheeling her shiny new bike up the driveway. Honey looked as hot and tired as Trixie felt, but her face was wreathed in smiles as she called out, "I can coast down our hill now without falling off. Watch me, Trixie. Watch me."

Trixie grinned as Honey turned the bike around and started down again. "Why, she's as excited as Bobby was when he learned to ride his trike," she thought. When Honey came back, she said with genuine admiration, "You're really marvelous. Tomorrow you'll be going down, no hands, no feet."

Honey's hazel eyes glowed, and with her red cheeks and sunburned nose, she didn't look at all like the pale, sick girl Trixie had met only a short time before. "The first time I tried it," she admitted to Trixie, "I was so scared I fell off before I even got started. The second time, I got as far as the bend in the driveway, and when I saw how far the road was I wanted to stop but I couldn't. And then, wouldn't you know it, a delivery truck turned into our driveway. I was shaking so I was sure I'd steer right into it the way I did at your house, but somehow, I wobbled past with just inches to spare." She laughed. "By the time I got to the bottom of the hill I was going so fast I couldn't stop and I couldn't turn, so I shot across the road and landed in the ditch on the other side." She patted her sore knee. "It was sure lucky I was wearing these pads your mother lent me."

"You're a wonder," Trixie said as they entered the big white house. "I wish I'd learned to ride a horse as fast as you learned to ride a bike."

"But you have, Trixie," Honey insisted. "Regan thinks you're terrific."

"I'll bet he does," Trixie said ruefully. "After what happened this morning!"

"He's not the least bit mad at *you,*" Honey said with a giggle, "but he gave *me* the dickens for letting you ride Jupe. He threatened to tell Dad and everything, but I knew he wouldn't."

The girls changed into bathing suits in Honey's room which was the prettiest room Trixie had ever seen. There were crisp white ruffled organdy curtains at the windows with a matching bedspread and a big white fluffy rug on the polished floor. The long closet was filled with dainty summer frocks, and beneath them, in individual cellophane boxes, were more shoes than Trixie had ever seen outside of a shoe store. Honey had her own private bathroom with a separate glassed-in shower and a sunken tub that was big enough to have served Bobby as a wading pool.

"I feel as though I were in a castle," Trixie said, in an awed voice. "I expect to see a fairy godmother any minute!"

Honey slipped into pale blue sharkskin shorts with a matching halter. "Sometime," she said shyly, "maybe you could spend the night with me. My bed's big enough for two, but if you'd rather you could sleep in one of the guest rooms."

"I'd rather be with you," Trixie said quickly. "That would be fun. And I know Moms would let me any time you ask me."

Down at the boathouse, Trixie, who didn't mind getting her short blond curls wet, dove off the diving board while Honey tucked her hair inside a bright red cap. Trixie floated on her back, luxuriating in the coolness of the water which was fed by icy springs. She watched Honey do a perfect jackknife off the board and cut cleanly through the water.

"Golly," she said as Honey swam beside her, "you do the crawl better than Mart, and you could give us all diving lessons!"

Honey smiled. "That's camp for you. There was never anything to do but swim and ride. I've been going to camp every summer since I was four, you know."

After a while they stretched out in the sun to dry off. As though by magic, a trim little maid in a crisp uniform and cap appeared with a tray of lemonade and a big chocolate layer cake.

"Do you realize," Honey demanded as she poured fruit juice into tall glasses of cracked ice, "that we have known each other only a couple of days? So much has happened it seems a month! Nothing ever happened to me till we moved to the Manor House. And to think, at first, I thought I was going to hate it!"

"It's a wonderful place," Trixie said, reaching hungrily for the large piece of freshly baked cake that Honey handed her. "I wish we owned it."

"Oh, no, you don't," Honey interrupted hastily. "Your little farmhouse is much cuter. It's got such a nice, cozy, lived-in feeling. This place is—well, as you said yourself—like a castle. I don't feel as though I belong here yet. But then, I felt the same way about our big duplex apartment in New York. It was just the place I stayed in, between camp and school." She added confidingly, "Mother doesn't like it here. I guess that's why Dad's taking her on a trip this evening. Mother likes to have a lot of people around all the time."

"Why, I've never even seen your mother," Trixie exclaimed wonderingly.

Honey flushed. "I know, and I want you to meet her as soon as they get back. She'll probably give a party and ask your mother and father. Mother was always giving parties in town or going out to them." She leaned forward a little, frowning. "I'm scared Mother won't stay here this winter, and I'll be sent away to school again! And, oh, gosh, Trixie, I want to stay here and go to school with you."

"I hope you do," Trixie said enthusiastically. "And wouldn't it be swell if old Mr. Frayne should get well and have Jim live with him? Then we could all go to school together."

Honey nodded and sucked thoughtfully at her glass straw. "I'm so afraid his uncle will die, and he'll have to go back to that awful Jonesy."

The girls sat in the boathouse for a while, thinking about Jim's problem, and then Trixie said, "We can't go in swimming right after eating, so let's row over to that cove on the other side of the lake. Brian and Mart and I always wanted to explore over there, but you can't get to it from the woods on our property because there's so much poison ivy."

"I don't know how to row," Honey objected.

"Neither do I." Trixie slid off the landing into the boat. "But all you do, I think, is push backward or forward with the oars. We can figure it out somehow."

Honey stepped in gingerly beside her. Trixie untied the boat and pushed it away from the landing. "I'll row," she said. "And I think you're supposed to sit in the stern. That's the other end," she added with a giggle, as Honey slipped past her and the boat rocked precariously. Honey sat down hard as Trixie put the oars into the oarlocks. At first they made very little headway, going mostly in circles; but, in a few minutes, Trixie had the boat under control and they rowed smoothly across the lake.

"It's easy as pie," she said as she guided the boat into the cove, "but I'm hot all over again, now. I'm going to dive right in and get cooled off," she added as she climbed onto a big flat rock.

"Be careful, Trixie," Honey cried. "It may be shallow here!"

But the warning came too late. As Trixie cut through the water, her legs scraped against the gravelly bottom. Then she felt a sharp pain in her head, and everything went black. When she opened her eyes again, she was sprawling upon the bank, half-in and half-out of the lake. The branches of the overhanging willow trees swayed dizzily above her, and she felt as though she were going to be sick. Her head ached as badly as it had when she'd had the measles, and when she drew her hand away from her cheek her fingers were sticky with blood. As the buzzing sound in her ears began to fade, she could hear Honey saying something in a voice that seemed very faraway.

Trixie closed her eyes to shut out the sight of the swaying branches and asked weakly, "What happened?"

Honey's voice came closer. "You must have hit your head on an underwater rock. It's only a few feet deep around here. I dragged you out by your hair. Do you feel better now?"

Trixie tried to nod her head but it had become too large and heavy to move. Gradually, the dizzy sensation left her, and she sat up, holding her throbbing head in both hands. "That was a dumb thing to do," she said sheepishly. "Diving off before I found out how deep it was."

Honey filled her bathing cap with water and washed the blood off Trixie's face. "It's not a very deep cut," she said, "but you're going to have a big bruise on your temple. It's already swelling."

Suddenly Trixie laughed. "Here I am all covered with blood and you're washing it off. How did it happen you didn't faint?"

"Gosh," Honey gasped in amazement. "That's right, I didn't. I guess I just didn't have time to think about it." She grinned. "I never felt less like fainting in my life. How do *you* feel?"

Trixie opened her mouth to say, "Better," when she caught a glimpse of something yellow skulking through the trees on the hill. "Oh, Honey!" she gasped. "There's that stray dog again. See him up there by the big oak?"

Honey stifled a scream. "He's coming down here. Oh, Trixie, what'll we do?"

Trixie stood up dizzily. The boat had floated away from the cove during the excitement, and she knew she was too weak to swim out after it. Honey stood frozen in her tracks, ankle deep in the water. Trixie gave her a little push. "You've got to get the boat," she ordered. "I can't make it, now. *You've got to!*"

She held her breath as Honey hesitated, then obediently plunged into the lake, flailing the water with her fast crawl strokes. Trixie lost sight of the dog for a moment, and then he appeared down on the path under the weeping willows. A mother duck quacked loudly to her babies and ushered them into the lake as the yellow dog slunk past.

Honey was pushing the rowboat back now, churning a wake behind her with her legs, and Trixie waded out to meet her. Her knees were knocking together from weakness and fright, and her head ached so she could hardly think. The dog hadn't gone after the ducks, she reasoned, so perhaps he couldn't swim. That was their only hope.

The boat scraped against the big, flat rock. "You get in first," Trixie ordered, holding it steady as Honey clambered over the side. "You've got to row." Somehow, she hoisted herself onto the rock.

Honey was trembling so she could hardly get the

oars in place. "Can you make it?" she asked over one shoulder. "Oh, Trixie, I can't row."

"You'll learn," Trixie said shortly as she slid from the rock into the stern.

The dog had caught sight of them now, and he broke into a run. With all the strength she could muster, Trixie leaned out and pushed the boat away from the rock. It shot out of the cove just as the ugly mongrel plunged off the path to the water's edge. He began to bark threateningly and leaped from the cove to the big flat rock.

Honey struggled desperately with the oars, too confused to follow Trixie's directions. The boat went round and round in what seemed like never-ending circles, getting nearer and nearer to the cove instead of away from it. "Suppose he can swim, Trixie," she wailed. "What'll we do?"

Chapter 9
Jim's Discovery

Trixie shuddered as she glanced swiftly at those dangerously close yellow eyes and savage jaws. "Hit him on the head with an oar, of course," she answered grimly. Suddenly, she remembered that Jim had said the dog was really a coward, and she crouched forward as she reached behind her for the rubber cushion on the stern seat. Then she threw it with all her might and main right into the dog's ugly face. The cur yelped in astonishment, lost his balance, and toppled backward with a loud splash into the shallow water. The bow of the boat bumped against the rock as the dog floundered to shore, shook himself, and darted off through the trees with his tail between his legs.

Trixie was too weak to move for a minute, and it was Honey who pushed the boat out of the cove with an oar. "You're simply wonderful, Trixie," she gasped.

Trixie splashed cold water on her face and felt better. "You're the real heroine," she said. "You went after the boat. I couldn't have made it."

"A lot of good that did," Honey insisted. "I've simply got to learn to row." She giggled as the boat began to move in circles again. "I think this thing is bewitched."

"I do, too." Trixie reached out and scooped up the rubber cushion as it floated past. "I'm getting dizzy all over again."

"That gives me an idea," Honey interrupted. "Let's name it the *Witch*. The *Water Witch*."

As though chastened, the *Water Witch* suddenly began to behave, and Honey rowed back across the lake without further trouble.

"Now it's your turn to put iodine on me," Trixie said as they climbed up the rustic steps from the boathouse.

Miss Trask met them on the wide veranda and supervised Honey's first-aid treatment. While they were changing into their clothes, Trixie said, "I know what let's do. Let's go down to your mailbox and see if the village paper has been delivered yet. The postman usually leaves it with the mail about this time of day. There might be something about old Mr. Frayne in it."

"But what about that dog?" Honey said hesitantly. "Won't he come back?"

"I'm not afraid of him any longer," Trixie answered. "He's a coward, just as Jim said. But let's take along a good strong stick or something."

Honey got two of her father's heavy walking sticks from the stand in the huge hall, and they hurried down the driveway.

On top of the mail in the Wheeler box was a copy of *The Sleepyside Sun*. Honey unfolded it quickly and gave a little gasp. Trixie peered over her shoulder and read:

JAMES WINTHROP FRAYNE
SERIOUSLY ILL

James Winthrop Frayne, 82, of Ten Acres, Glen Road, is seriously ill of pneumonia. Mr. Frayne, who was one of the founders of the Sleepyside Hospital, was found yesterday morning, unconscious at the foot of his driveway by a neighbor, Mr. Peter Belden, employee of the First National Bank. Mr. Belden drove the aged man to the hospital where his condition was pronounced serious. Today doctors said Mr. Frayne was failing rapidly. Authorities are making every effort to locate and notify Mr. Frayne's relatives, but so far no record of any living relative has been found.

"Honey," Trixie said, "we'd better tell Jim about this right away. If the story gets into the New York papers, the place will be swarming with reporters."

"Oh, I don't think it's important enough for that," Honey said dubiously.

"You never can tell," Trixie insisted. "If a New York paper heard the story about half a million dollars being hidden up there, they'd send photographers out, and when they saw all those piles of junk, the story would be all over the front page."

"Well, maybe so," Honey admitted. "But I honestly don't believe that story and neither does Jim."

"I do," Trixie said stubbornly. Her concern about Jim had made her forget her aching head for a few minutes as she continued, "And, anyway, Jim ought to try to find a will or something. I'm going straight up there now and tell him he really ought to search the place thoroughly while he still has a chance."

Honey stuck the paper back in the mailbox. "I'll come with you, but don't you have to water your garden?"

"Oh," Trixie moaned, "I forgot all about that."

"I'll help," Honey offered.

Later, as they filled two big watering cans at the cistern, Trixie complained, "This is almost the worst part of having a garden. I wish it would rain. Everything's so dry around here if anyone dropped a lighted match on a leaf we'd have a regular forest fire."

"I know," Honey said as they trudged down to the

garden. "Jim was talking about that this morning when he was being very careful to put out every spark of the fire he built outside. He was also kind of worried that someone might see the smoke and investigate."

"Well, he needn't worry about that," Trixie panted as she sloshed water on the pepper plants. "There's not another place around here except yours and ours for acres and acres. But he'd better be careful inside that crumbling old house with all that paper lying around. If a fire ever started there, no one would ever be able to stop it."

They walked slowly back and refilled their watering cans. "The cistern's almost empty," Trixie said. "It went dry one summer when a fire started down in our field below the garden. There aren't any hydrants around here, you know, so, although they sent out the whole fire department, the chemical truck was the only one they could use. They got the fire under control pretty quickly," she went on, "but the chief told Dad that if the wind had been blowing in the other direction our house would have caught fire before they could have stopped it. We've been awfully careful about matches ever since then, and Dad won't even let Brian burn the trash now."

Honey glanced up at the old house on the hill.

"Gosh," she murmured, "if the Mansion caught fire, it might spread through the woods to our house and yours, mightn't it?"

"That's right," Trixie said. "And in this dry weather all three of them would probably burn to the ground."

When the last row of plants had been watered, the girls put the cans and garden tools in the garage and started up the hill.

"I'm so tired I can hardly move," Honey said as she trailed farther and farther behind. "I guess I'm just not used to so much exercise. I've simply got to rest a minute or I'll drop in my tracks."

"Okay," Trixie said, "but come on just as soon as you can."

She whistled as she pushed through the thicket, and in a minute or two Jim appeared at the window. "Hi," he called out. "Didn't expect to see you until tomorrow."

"I've got bad news," Trixie panted. "Your uncle's dying, Jim. It was in the afternoon paper."

Jim looked serious. "That's too bad. I wish I dared risk going in to see him. I'm his only living relative, you know."

"You mustn't," Trixie objected. "The police or some-body would want to know where you're living and all about you. They'd be sure to notify Jonesy then, wouldn't they?"

Jim nodded thoughtfully. "Just the same, I hate to think of Uncle James dying in a hospital all alone."

"I think we ought to search some more for that money," Trixie insisted. "He may die without telling anyone where it is."

"I have searched." Jim reached inside for the shotgun he had been cleaning and, dangling his long legs over the sill, began polishing the barrel with a piece of oily rag. "I've given all the downstairs a thorough going-over," he went on. "I've even rapped the living-room panels from floor to ceiling looking for a secret hiding place." He grinned. "And don't ask me because I looked: there's not a single sign of a trap door in the cellar."

Trixie sat down on the sparse grass beneath the window. She suddenly felt as exhausted as Honey had a few minutes before. "There must be a will, or at least a letter, around somewhere which would tell where the money's hidden," she said crossly. "How about that desk?"

Jim shook his head. "I found the key to the desk. It was hanging on a ring with a bunch of others on a nail behind the cellar door. There was nothing in the desk but some pass books to several New York savings banks."

"Well, my goodness," Trixie exclaimed excitedly. "That's something, anyway. You're the heir, so all the money in those banks will belong to you when your uncle dies."

Jim loaded the gun before he replied. "All those accounts had been closed out years ago, Trixie," he said quietly. "I'm afraid that proves more than ever that Uncle James spent or lost all his money."

Trixie sighed. "I think we really ought to search the top floor, Jim. Right away. If your uncle dies, the story may be written up in the New York papers, and then there'll be a lot of reporters snooping around here, and we may never have another chance."

Jim looked startled. "If it gets in the papers, Jonesy will come snooping around," he said slowly.

"Well, then," Trixie cried triumphantly. "Let's get going. Is there a ladder in the barn?"

Jim frowned. "I don't like the idea. It seems like prying into something my uncle didn't want anyone to see."

"Why *must* you be so stubborn?" Trixie demanded. "I don't see what difference it makes. If you searched one floor, why not another? Anyway, the whole place really belongs to you now, Jim!"

"Not exactly," he said. "Uncle James isn't dead yet, and he might have changed his will, you know."

"Oh, for heaven's sakes," Trixie groaned. "Let's try to find the will then." She added ominously, "If nobody ever finds it, you'll have to go back to your stepfather."

Jim's face darkened. "I told you I'd never go back," he said hotly. "I can get a job at a summer camp."

"And what about afterward?" Trixie goaded him. "You don't want to quit school now. Not with only one more year to go and a scholarship for college waiting for you."

"I do want to go to college," Jim admitted ruefully. "I'd like to get at least a master's degree so I could teach the boys some subjects myself if that dream of mine ever comes true."

Trixie knew he was weakening now. "This old house is worthless, I guess," she said quickly, "but land around here sells for a thousand dollars an acre. So you'll inherit at least ten thousand dollars when your uncle dies. *If,*" she finished pointedly, "we find the will."

"I guess you're right." Jim turned to put the gun inside the house but stopped suddenly. "Listen," he whispered. "Something's running along the bridle trail from the Wheeler place."

"What of it?" Trixie demanded sourly. "It's probably Reddy chasing a squirrel or a chipmunk."

"It *sounds* like a dog," Jim said, still listening. "But it's running like crazy and—"

At that moment Honey emerged from the driveway.

"Hello," she called out. "At the last minute, I was too scared of Queenie to go through the thicket alone so I came up this way." She stopped as she noticed Jim's tense face. "What's the matter?"

Trixie could hear the animal now, racing up the path on the other side of the hedge; and, as Honey's face turned white, Trixie realized that she had heard it, too. Whatever it was, it tore ahead, straight into the thicket. *It's not Reddy,* Trixie thought wildly. *He would have turned off at the downtrail to our house.*

There was the sound of something thrashing madly in the tangled vines, and then the yellow mongrel burst into the clearing. Foam was dripping from its vicious muzzle, and Honey screamed once as it plunged onward, straight at her.

Chapter 10
The Old Ladder

"Stand still, Honey!" Jim yelled as he raised his gun to his shoulder and fired.

The dog leaped convulsively into the air, then dropped dead, not two feet from where Honey was standing. Honey had covered her face with her hands, and she pitched forward into their arms as Jim and Trixie raced to her side.

"She's fainted," Trixie yelled as they carefully lowered her to the ground.

Jim raced around to the well in the back of the house and returned with a tin can full of water. Then, for the second time that day, Trixie bathed Honey's face and wrists. The icy cold water brought Honey to immediately, and she sat up with a little moan.

"My nightmare!" she exclaimed, looking first at one and then the other. "It was just like a dream. I couldn't run."

"It was a good thing you didn't," Jim said. "In the first place, it's never wise to run away from a dog, anyway. It confuses them if you stand perfectly still and show no sign of fear. And in the second place, if you had run toward us, you would have got between me and the dog, so I couldn't have shot it." He stared soberly down at the dead animal. "Poor old fellow. I had hopes of making friends with him sometime and trying to tame him, but I guess he's better off this way. I wouldn't have been able to take him with me when I go."

"Jim," Honey asked impulsively, "you're not going away soon, are you?"

Jim shrugged noncommittally as he dragged the dog into the field to bury it.

Trixie and Honey rested in the shade while they waited for Jim to return. Honey was still weak from fright and was glad of the chance to lie quietly in the shade for a few minutes.

When he came back, Honey asked, "Do you think he had rabies, Jim?"

"I don't think so," Jim said. "Dogs often froth at the mouth in hot weather or because of nervousness."

"I know," Trixie put in. "When Reddy was a puppy he used to when he was carsick."

Honey shuddered. "But suppose he *had* had hydrophobia and had bitten me, I would have died, wouldn't I?"

"Oh, no," Jim said easily. "There's the Pasteur treatment, you know. Your doctor would have immediately vaccinated you against hydrophobia." He smiled at Honey sympathetically. "You had a nasty scare. Feel all right now?"

Honey nodded. "But I'm glad that dog won't bother us any more." They told him, then, about Trixie's accident and how she had thrown the cushion in the mongrel's face.

"I was wondering where you got that bump." Jim grinned admiringly at Trixie. "It took plenty of nerve to do what you did, but it took a heck of a lot more to do what you did yesterday. You have plenty of courage."

Trixie flushed uncomfortably. "I don't know what you mean."

"Sucking the venom out of Bobby's toe," he explained. "If you'd had a cut or a sore in your mouth—"

"I never even thought about that," Trixie admitted.

"If we're going to do a lot of roaming through these woods and fields," Jim said thoughtfully, "we really ought to carry snake-bite kits. They come equipped with a scalpel, suction pump, and tourniquet, you know. The important thing with snake bites is speed and keeping the victim quiet, so the poison won't spread. But the *most* important thing," he finished, "is to avoid being bitten. And you, Trixie, ought to be more careful. You were all set to barge into that summerhouse this morning. Don't you know that snakes love to rest in deserted houses?"

Trixie stared, shamefaced, down at her hands, and Honey quickly changed the subject. "Whatever happened to Queenie?"

"She's okay," Jim told her. "I saw her tearing across the courtyard just before you came up. She just pretended to be hurt, the way wild birds do, to lure the dog away from where her nest is hidden in the thicket."

"I'm glad of that," Trixie said. "She's a wonderful little hen. I was wondering how we were ever going to catch her so we could put a splint on her wing. She scurries away at the first sound of anyone coming near."

"We would have had to do it at night," Jim said. "*If* we could have found her nest. And I doubt if we could have done that."

"Wait till you see her baby chicks," Trixie told Honey. "They're the cutest little balls of yellow fluff with stripes down their backs like chipmunks."

"I'd love to see one," Honey said. "But I wouldn't dare go near them."

"You wouldn't have a chance," Trixie said. "If you think Queenie's mean while she's setting, you ought to see her after the eggs are hatched. Boy! She's a terror."

She turned to Jim. "Come on, it's getting late. Aren't we going to explore the top floor?"

"Okay," Jim said reluctantly as he led the way around to the barn in the back of the house. "But I still don't like the idea."

"I don't either," Honey said determinedly. "I wouldn't go up there for anything in the whole wide world."

"What's that?" Trixie asked, pointing to an oil drum which hung from a branch of a large evergreen.

Jim grinned. "That's my outdoor shower. I got so hot and dirty looking for hidden treasure I rigged it up."

"How does it work?" Trixie demanded.

"Well, first I punched a hole in the bottom of the drum and ran a rope through it, knotting one end and looping the other over the branch. Then I punched a lot of little holes around the big one. After that all you have to do is fill the can with water, pull on the rope, and stand under your shower."

"Why, it's wonderful," Trixie cried. "I'm going to make one for Bobby. He'll love it! He's always begging me to squirt him with the hose."

"Down at your place," Jim said, "you probably have a hose, so you can make a permanent shower. Tie the can securely in the fork of the tree, place one end of the hose in it, turn on the water, and there you are. But," he cautioned, "you'd better not waste water until we get a good long rain. The well up here is almost dry."

"Our brook is nothing but a trickle," Trixie said. "I wish it would rain. With the cistern so low, we're going to have to bring water soon from the house to the garden, and that's an awful chore. I don't like to carry heavy water buckets."

They found an old cobwebby ladder in the barn and dragged it around to the house. The girls held the ladder in place while Jim tried one second-story window after another without success, for the windows had apparently not been opened for years.

"Of course they're all locked," Trixie said in disgust. "Nobody would be dumb enough to board up the staircase without first locking all the windows up there."

"Well, I'm not going to break in," Jim said stubbornly. "And," he finished, "I won't have to. This one's stuck but not locked. I can pry it loose with a hammer and chisel."

"Great!" Trixie cried. "I can hardly wait to see what's up there."

Jim started down backward and halfway to the ground there was a rending, splintering sound as one rung in the old ladder split in two under Jim's weight. He struggled wildly to regain his balance, and, although the girls used all their combined strength to hold the ladder in place, it swung slowly but surely away from the wall.

It seemed like hours that it swayed in midair and then crashed to the ground, pinning Jim beneath its weight.

Chapter 11
A Precious Piece of Paper

"Oh, oh," Honey shrieked. "His back's broken. I know it is!"

Trixie felt a scream rising in her own throat as she stared dazedly at the crumpled form of the boy. Every freckle stood out in the whiteness of his face, and his hair was a bright splotch of red against his pale forehead. Then, as he let out an involuntary moan, she began tugging at the heavy ladder. Between them, the girls finally lifted and pushed the ladder away, and Jim looked up with a sickly grin.

"Golly, I know now what a drowning man goes through," he said. "Everything that ever happened to me flashed through my mind while that ladder was deciding what it was going to do." He stretched his arms and legs tentatively, slowly flexing his wrists and ankles. "No bones broken, thank goodness." He sat up. "I made myself go limp as soon as I realized I was going to fall."

"I was pretty limp myself," Trixie said, and grinned.

Jim scrambled to his feet, rubbing the back of his

head. "I'll have a lump the size of yours," he told Trixie. "It was lucky I didn't crack my skull." He laughed ruefully. "Jonesy always said I was hardheaded, and I guess he's right."

"That makes three of us," Honey declared. "First I cut my knee, then Trixie hit her head on a rock, and now you topple off a ladder. What's going to happen next?"

"Nothing," Trixie said. "Bad things always go in threes, so the jinx is over."

"I'm not so sure of that." Honey was counting on her fingers. "Jupiter ran away with you. I almost got run over by the laundry truck, and the dog chased us down the lake."

"Well, that's just another set of threes," Jim said cheerfully.

"How about the dog running after me a little while ago?" Honey demanded. "Doesn't that start off still another set?"

Trixie shrugged. "Have it your way. Two more awful things are going to happen to us."

Honey looked hurt and said quietly, "What I'm trying to say is that I don't think Jim ought to climb up that ladder again today. He might get dizzy after such a bad fall."

"You're right." Jim shook his head vigorously. "I can

still hear bells ringing in my ears. Anyway, the light's fading. It'll be pitch black up there with the windows as coated with dirt as they are. We wouldn't be able to see a thing."

"That's right." Trixie was sorry she had made fun of Honey. "I really ought to go home and help Mother with supper. I'll bring up a couple of flashlights, and we can explore tomorrow morning."

As the girls strolled down the path to the hollow, Honey said, "I know you think I'm silly to be so superstitious, but—"

"I don't," Trixie interrupted hastily. "I'm pretty superstitious myself. I wouldn't walk under a ladder for anything, and as for black cats!" She laughed. "One ran across the road in front of our car once, and Dad went into a ditch trying to avoid it. He broke a spring, so now we're all superstitious about black cats."

"It's more than that with me," Honey said solemnly. "I just have the most peculiar feeling that something awful's going to happen. I don't really believe in premonitions or dreams, but, after all, I had a nightmare about something attacking me and something did."

Trixie glanced at her curiously. "That's so," she admitted. "What's this peculiar feeling like? What do you think's going to happen?"

Honey shivered. "I don't know. But it's connected with that creepy old house, somehow. All the time I'm up there, I feel like looking over my shoulder to see what's behind me. It's horrid, and I suppose it's just because I'm such a sissy, but—"

"You're not a sissy," Trixie broke in. "I wish you'd stop saying that all the time. I think you're great. Honest. I never heard of anyone going down such a steep hill on a bike the very first day, and the way you swam after that boat when your knees must have been knocking together the way mine were. By the way," she finished, "how *is* that knee of yours?"

"Oh, oh," Honey said. "I forgot to put another bandage on it after we went in swimming."

"Well, don't forget to put one on tomorrow morning," Trixie said as she stopped at the mailbox at the end of the driveway. "And you'd better wear a knee pad, too, if we're going in for the papers."

Bobby was well enough to sit up and play checkers with his father on Sunday morning. "Hurry up and bring back the funnies," he ordered Trixie from the window as she and Honey set off on their bikes.

The girls stopped long enough at the little Glen Road store to examine the New York papers thoroughly, and they were relieved to find no mention in them of old

Mr. Frayne. Trixie introduced Honey to the storekeeper.

"Her family just bought the Manor House on the hill above ours, Mr. Lytell," she explained.

"Is that so?" Mr. Lytell pushed his glasses farther up his nose. "Hear your other neighbor, Mr. Frayne, is pretty sick, Trixie."

"I guess he's dying," Trixie said and started to move away.

"Just a minute." The storekeeper came out from behind the counter. "You girls had better pick up a stick on the way home. There's a stray dog loose around here. A mean-looking cur. Saw him early the other morning when I was riding my old nag through the woods across the road from your place, Trixie. Saw something else, too." He took off his glasses and began polishing them with his handkerchief. "Smoke rising from the Mansion. You girls aren't fooling around up there building camp-fires, are you? That old wreck would burn like dry timber if it caught fire."

He looked up suddenly, and Trixie knew her face was bright red. "Oh, no, Mr. Lytell," she said hastily. "I wouldn't light a match anywhere in the woods or fields after the fire we had summer before last."

He looked at her suspiciously and grunted. "Smoke doesn't rise by itself."

141

"Whew!" Trixie gasped as they got on their bikes. "I forgot all about Mr. Lytell. We'd better warn Jim not to build any more fires."

"It's lucky he thought it was us," Honey said. "Otherwise, he might have investigated and discovered Jim."

They coasted down the hill to the Belden driveway, Trixie riding no hands, no feet. "At the rate you're going, you'll be doing this yourself as soon as your knee heals," she told Honey.

"Well, I'm not going to try it for a long time," Honey said. "So much happened yesterday I'm beginning to think it must have been Friday the thirteenth." She waited in the garage where they parked their bikes while Trixie brought the papers down to the terrace where Mr. and Mrs. Belden were having coffee.

"I'll take the comics up to Bobby," she said. "Then, can I fool around with Honey till lunchtime?"

Mrs. Belden nodded. "It's much too hot to work in the garden."

"You've been doing a good job with the chickens, Trixie," her father said. "And you deserve a day off; but I'd like to take your mother for a drive this afternoon, so will you sit with Bobby?"

"Sure, Dad." Trixie hurried into the house and upstairs.

Bobby was blowing bubbles through a straw into his grape juice, but he handed the glass to Trixie and pounced upon the comics.

As she was leaving the room, Trixie picked up the flashlight which was on the top of the bookshelf.

"Hey!" Bobby howled. "Where're you going with my flashlight? You put that right back, Trixie Belden. You wouldn't let me play with the one you got for your birthday, so I won't let you play with mine."

"It's not yours," Trixie said impatiently. "It's Dad's. And I'm not going to play with it. I just want to borrow it for a little while."

"Is so mine. Daddy said so last night," Bobby insisted loudly and petulantly. "Hey! I know where you're going. You're going off 'sploring again."

"Sh-h!" Trixie put a warning finger to her lips.

Bobby threw himself back on the pillows, wailing at the top of his lungs: "I wanna go 'sploring, too. My toe's all better now. I don't wanna stay here in bed. I wanna go *'sploring!*"

Trixie could hear her mother hurrying up the stairs to see why Bobby was crying, and she whispered desperately, "Please be quiet, Bobby. If you're quiet, I'll read the funnies to you all afternoon. Promise."

Immediately, the little boy's plump face was

wreathed in smiles. "It's a see-crud, isn't it, Trixie? Your see-crud and my see-crud. But you gotta read *Peter Rabbit* to me three times or I'll tell."

"All *right,*" Trixie promised as she hurried out of the room.

"Lunch at one-thirty," Mrs. Belden called after her. "And don't be late. I'm roasting a turkey."

"Gosh," Trixie groaned as she joined Honey in the garage. "Bobby was on the verge of telling Moms we're exploring the Miser's Mansion. I had to promise to read to him all afternoon to keep him quiet."

"What a shame," Honey said sympathetically. "That means you can't go riding with Jim and me."

Trixie tried to shrug away her disappointment. "It doesn't matter. You two will have more fun without me until I learn to ride better."

"That's not true," Honey broke in generously. "You're doing very well, Trixie. Regan told me this morning that you'd be ready for jumping in another week or two."

"Golly." Trixie stopped in the middle of the path, so thrilled she could hardly speak. "Do you really think he meant it, Honey?" she asked humbly.

"Of course. Regan's like your mother," she said, laughing. "He never says anything he doesn't mean."

Jim answered their whistle from the barn and came out dragging the ladder. "I got the window open the first thing this morning," he told them. "But I put the ladder away in case somebody came snooping around."

Trixie told him then that Mr. Lytell had seen the smoke from his fire. "That's one more reason why we should find that will right away," she finished. "He may come up here, after all, to investigate."

"That's true," Jim said thoughtfully. "And I suppose there must be a will somewhere. Or at least a deed to the property. Of course, it may be mortgaged to the hilt."

"Have you looked around up there already?" Trixie asked.

Jim grinned. "No, I knew you'd have a fit if I didn't wait for you. Anyway, it's so dark I couldn't have seen anything."

Trixie handed him a second flashlight that she had picked up in the garage.

"I don't see why this house hasn't got electric lights," Honey remarked. "If Mr. Frayne was as rich as he was supposed to be, you'd think he would have had the place wired."

"It's wired all right," Jim said as he started up the

ladder, "but he probably had the current shut off at the time that he went into retirement. That's why there's no running water, either. The pump in the basement runs by electricity." At the top of the ladder, Jim played the flashlight around inside the house. "This was somebody's bedroom," he called down to the girls. "My aunt's, I guess, and it doesn't look as though it's been touched since the day she died." He disappeared through the window.

"I'll hold the ladder for you, Trixie," Honey offered. "After what happened to Jim yesterday, I wouldn't climb up this rickety old thing for all the treasure in the world."

When Trixie hoisted herself over the window sill, she turned on her own torch. She found herself in what had once been a luxurious bedroom, but the dusty silk drapes were hanging in shreds from the rusty rods, and the bedspread had almost completely rotted away. Squirrels and field mice had played havoc with the rich upholstery of the furniture, and strips of faded wallpaper were crumbling to a yellow powder on the floor. In the long, glass-doored closet were the discolored remnants of a woman's wardrobe, fashionable more than ten years ago.

"It's really a crime," Trixie said to Jim, "that your

uncle let this place go to rack and ruin. Why, if that Oriental rug hadn't been eaten to pieces by moths, it would be absolutely priceless."

She followed him through a connecting bath into the master bedroom. The beautiful mahogany of the huge four-poster bed was white with mold, and spider webs almost completely covered the Chippendale desk in one corner of the room. They peered into the closets and drawers and shook their heads over the moth-eaten suits and the shirts and underclothing which nesting rodents had gnawed to rags.

"I don't get it," Trixie said in an awed voice. "The only time I ever saw your uncle he was wearing such a funny-looking, patched outfit he looked like a scarecrow."

Jim played his light along the rows of empty bookshelves and stopped to stare a moment at the dried-up body of a baby bird in the ashes of the fireplace. "I guess the desk is our best bet," he said as he combed away the cobwebs with a coat-hanger.

Trixie hung excitedly over his shoulder and sighed in disappointment when he pulled down the flap. There was nothing but dust in the pigeonholes, and the drawers were empty except for a few rusty penpoints and paper clips.

"I imagine that's the answer," Jim said, pointing his torch to the ashes in the grate. "He must have burned everything before he boarded up the staircase."

"I won't give up," Trixie said stubbornly, "until we've looked into every nook and cranny of this floor and the attic."

But there was nothing of value in either the guest rooms or the sewing room, and the low-ceilinged attic was completely bare. At the end of a hot, dusty, discouraging hour even Trixie was willing to give up.

"No will, no nothing," she told Honey as she climbed backward down the ladder. "I guess that crazy old miser must have burned everything."

"You were up there so long I was beginning to be afraid something had happened. Be careful of that missing rung," Honey cautioned.

Jim appeared at the window with a big, black book in his hand. "I thought I might as well bring this old Bible along," he said as he started down. "It was on a bedside table in one of the guest rooms. I haven't any other family possessions except my mug, so I don't think Uncle James would mind my having it."

"Watch out for the broken place," both Trixie and Honey cried together. And then they dodged as the heavy Bible slipped from Jim's hand and hurtled past their heads. A piece of paper flew from the pages of the book and landed at Trixie's feet. She leaned over to pick it up.

"Golly, golly!" she shouted. "It's a will, Jim. *The will!*"

Chapter 12
Jed Tomlin's Colt

Trixie handed the yellowed legal paper to Jim. "Read it quickly," she begged. "Are you the heir? The sole heir?"

Jim read the will carefully before he answered. "Yes, I am, if this is the latest will. It's only a copy. It says here that a Mr. George Rainsford is the executor; so I imagine he has the original. Do you know who he is, Trixie?"

Trixie shook her head. "Never heard of him."

"He might very well be dead by now," Jim said. "This will was drawn up right after my aunt died when Uncle James was still rich."

"I still think he is rich," Trixie said firmly.

"Well," Jim said slowly, "the only person who would know about that would be Mr. Rainsford."

"George Rainsford," Honey repeated to herself. "That name sounds sort of familiar to me."

Jim slipped the will back into the Bible with a rueful chuckle. "I'm heir apparent to ten thousand dollars' worth of land, but it won't do me any good until I'm twenty-one. There won't be anything left by then—

Jonesy'll see to that. If only I could have got here a day earlier! Uncle James would, at least, have told me whether or not Mr. Rainsford is still alive, and he might even have tried to have another guardian appointed."

"Don't give up hope," Honey begged. "Your uncle isn't dead yet. Maybe he'll pull through after all."

Jim shrugged. "I doubt it. Not at his age. But I'll stick around here a few more days, just in case."

Trixie felt a huge lump rising in her throat. "And then what?" she got out.

"And then I'll start looking for a job." The boy's broad shoulders drooped disconsolately. "There goes college and my dream, but it can't be helped. I wouldn't live another year with Jonesy for all the money in the world."

"Oh, you mustn't quit school now!" Honey was on the verge of tears. "Please wait till Dad gets back from Canada next week, and let me tell him the whole story. Maybe his lawyers can do something."

"I wouldn't risk it," Jim said soberly. "The first thing your father would feel he had to do would be to notify Jonesy. And then I'd be right back where I started."

Abruptly, he turned away as though he wanted to be alone with his problem, and the girls started down the hill as he put away the ladder.

"We've got to do something," Trixie said mournfully.

"I hate to think of Jim wandering around the country without any money. And I'm not too sure he can get a job at a boys' camp without his stepfather's permission. Dad wrote several letters and went to see the head of the camp where Brian and Mart are before it was all settled."

"I know," Honey agreed. "Jim realizes that. And you know what? He told me if he had any trouble, he'd get a job on a cattle boat. If he does that, we may never see him again." She sighed. "I like Jim an awful lot, Trixie. I like him just as much as if he were my own brother. I wish we could fix things so Dad could adopt him."

"I wish so, too." She tossed a pebble into the woods. "I think we ought to keep right on looking for that money. I've got one of your premonitions about it. I'm sure it's there somewhere, and I don't think Jim really looked hard, enough, because he doesn't believe in it."

"He couldn't possibly have gone through every one of those boxes and barrels in such a short time," Honey agreed. "Let's all give the downstairs another thorough search tomorrow."

"Great!" Trixie waved good-by as Honey got on her bicycle. "Have fun on your ride this afternoon."

"Thanks," Honey called over her shoulder. "See you tomorrow."

Trixie's parents were upstairs with Bobby when she got home. From the downstairs hall, Trixie could hear her father's voice droning on and on, so she guessed that he was probably reading Bobby to sleep.

While Trixie stood there listening, her mother came quietly down the stairs with a tray of empty dishes. "Sh-h," she whispered to Trixie as they went out into the kitchen. "Bobby's had his lunch, and I think he'll fall asleep in a few minutes. A good long nap would do him a world of good."

Trixie nodded. "If anyone can read him to sleep, it's Dad. I can remember when I was Bobby's age and had mumps and measles, he used to tell me stories or read to me. His voice is so soothing, I used to fall into sort of a stupor right away, although I tried like anything not to." She gave her mother an impulsive hug. "Oh, Moms, I'm so glad I was born into this family. I feel so sorry for people like Honey and Ji—" She stopped herself just in time, and added hastily: "Honey just never seems to have any fun with her father and mother the way Bobby and Brian and Mart and I do. I'm so glad we're not rich."

"So am I," Mrs. Belden said with a smile. "It's much more fun to work for the things you want than to have them given to you on a silver platter. Speaking of which," she added with a chuckle, "will you rinse and dry our silver platter? Dad will be down in a few minutes to carve the turkey."

"Yummy-yum," Trixie said sniffing. "It smells dee-licious, Moms. I hope you put a lot of onions in the stuffing."

"I did," Mrs. Belden said as she took a big green glass bowl from the cupboard. "Let's not bother with cooked vegetables. If we eat all we want of the turkey and stuffing we won't have room for more than a tossed green salad."

"Yummy-yum," Trixie said again, in full agreement. "You fix that special salad dressing of yours, Moms, and I'll slice tomatoes and peppers and leeks and shred the lettuce."

"Fine," Mrs. Belden said. "We make a good team, Trixie. While we work, please tell me more about your new friend. I'm very interested in Honey. I think she's a lovely girl, but, of course, I don't know her as well as you do."

"She *is* just lovely in every way," Trixie cried enthusiastically. "I wasn't crazy about her at first, Moms. I thought she was a sissy. But she isn't. She's scared and nervous about a lot of things because she isn't used to living in the country. I mean, she's sure that every rope-like vine is a snake and all leaves are poison ivy, and things like that. And, of course, not having had any brothers makes an awful difference." Trixie scooped the core and seeds out of a big green pepper and began to slice it on the wooden chopping board. "I guess I never realized before," she said thoughtfully, "how important brothers are. Brian and Mart drive me wild sometimes because they're forever teasing me, and Bobby, well, he's darling but he can be an—an—"

"An awful nuisance," Mrs. Belden finished cheerfully. "But, Trixie, if you ever had to be separated from him for very long, you'd find that you missed him dreadfully. Brian and Mart have found that out while they've been at camp. With every letter they write me they enclose a note full of funny drawings for Bobby."

"I know," Trixie said. "Oh, Moms, let's not tell them about Bobby and the copperhead. Brian and Mart would just die from worry, and the worst is over now. He really is going to be all right, isn't he, Moms?"

"He's fine," Trixie's mother said emphatically. "And all due to you, Trixie. No. I'm sorry, but I'm not going to keep Bobby's accident a secret from Brian and Mart, Trixie. I'm going to write them a long letter telling them what an important part you played. They'll be very proud of you."

Trixie's father came tiptoeing into the kitchen then.

"Whew!" he sighed, "I thought His Royal Highness would never give up and close those big blue eyes of his." He washed his hands at the kitchen sink and then he deftly transferred the turkey from the oven pan to the gleaming silver platter. He winked at Trixie and said, "If there's one thing I like better than turkey with your mother's onion stuffing, it's more turkey with more stuffing. Let's eat right here in the kitchen."

"I'd like that," Mrs. Belden said gaily. "And I'm sure Trixie would, too. She's going to have to clean up when we leave for our drive and listen every now and then at the bottom of the stairs, too, to make sure Bobby is still asleep. I'm all in favor of saving unnecessary steps during an emergency like this."

She and Trixie set the kitchen table while Mr. Belden carved. It was much more cozy than eating in the dining-room, and in between mouthfuls, Trixie told her parents about her riding lessons.

"Regan says I'm doing very well," she finished. "Honey told me this morning that he'd probably let me do some jumping in another couple of weeks."

"Fine," her father said—"but don't rush things, Trixie. We don't want another invalid around here until Bobby is back on his feet." He grinned. "Although I suppose that imp is really less trouble when he's in bed than he is when he's running around loose, getting into mischief every step he takes."

"For your sake, Trixie," Mrs. Belden added, "I hope Bobby sleeps all afternoon. But if he does wake up around three, you might give him some pineapple juice and a few cookies. He didn't eat much lunch." She went upstairs then to take off her cotton house frock and don a cool, white sharkskin suit.

"I want your mother to get a change of scene," Mr. Belden said to Trixie. "Bobby has kept her pretty tied down. We'll drive up the river and have tea somewhere on the road. It'll do her good."

"I know," Trixie agreed as she rinsed the dishes and stacked them in the sink. "Don't hurry back, Dad. I'll keep Bobby good and quiet. After we've read the comics we can cut out the animals and play games with them. He likes that."

Trixie waved good-by to her parents from the terrace, then she tidied up the kitchen, washed and dried the dishes. She had hardly finished putting the last fork away in the silver drawer when Bobby woke up and yelled at the top of his lungs:

"I'm thirsty—and *hung*-gry! Holp!"

"Okay, Bobby," Trixie called up to him. "I'll be with you in a sec." Hastily she put a glass of pineapple juice and a plate of chocolate cookies on a tray and hurried upstairs.

Bobby greeted her with a fretful frown. "Straws," he said disdainfully. "You know I *have* to have straws."

Trixie laughed. "Here's a whole box of colored straws which your friend, Miss Trask, sent you. Red, green, blue, yellow, every color in the rainbow, Bobby. Take your choice."

Bobby squealed with delight. "I'll take a norange one *and* a labbender one," he said happily. "Labbender is sometimes almost always my very favrit color."

As he munched cookies and sipped the ice-cold juice, Bobby insisted upon hearing what Trixie and Honey had discovered up at the old Mansion.

"Nothing much," Trixie replied evasively. "The rooms are all filled with piles of junk. You can see it through the windows," she added quickly, so that Bobby wouldn't guess they had gone inside the house. You never could tell how long Bobby could keep a secret, and Trixie wasn't at all sure, now, that her father would approve of her having climbed in through the window that first day. "He'd probably give me the dickens," she reflected, "even though I did it just to lock up the place."

She picked up *Peter Rabbit* and began to read, but Bobby interrupted.

"What'd you want the flashlight for, Trixie?" he demanded suspiciously. "Did you find a pirate's cave or something?"

Trixie laughed. "No, of course not, Bobby. Don't you want me to read?"

Bobby shook his head up and down.

"Well, then, stop interrupting."

"I want to know why you borrowed my flashlight," the little boy insisted, his red lips beginning to pout. "You said it was my see-crud and your see-crud, but you won't tell me *anything!*"

Trixie sighed. "All right, but you've got to promise to keep this secret."

"I *always* keep see-cruds," Bobby boasted.

"Oh, no, you don't," Trixie corrected him. "Remember when I showed you the present I got for Mummy last Christmas? You promised not to let her guess what it was, so I could surprise her, and then that night when she was hearing you say your prayers, you said, 'And please, God, don't let me tell Mummy that Trixie bought her bedroom slippers for Christmas.'"

"That was different," Bobby said, squirming with embarrassment. "I was just a little boy then. I'm all growed up now."

"Well, then," Trixie went on reluctantly, "I'll tell you

what we discovered. The old summerhouse. It's all covered over with vines and branches. When you're well, I'll take you up there and show it to you."

Bobby flung himself back on the pillows, sulking with disappointment. "What's so 'citing about an old summerhouse?" he demanded petulantly. "Go on, *read!*"

After Trixie had been reading for what seemed like hours, Bobby dropped off to sleep. During this short nap, Trixie fed and watered the chickens and gathered the eggs. She was putting them away when her parents returned.

"Sh-h," she cautioned them. "The Little King is asleep. I'm practically hoarse from reading to him, but he was as good as gold."

Mrs. Belden smiled. "He's always good with you, Trixie. That is, when you don't lose your patience, as you sometimes do."

Mr. Belden patted Trixie's shoulder approvingly. "Keep on the way you're going, Trixie," he said, "and you'll surely have a horse next year. We ran into Jed Tomlin at the Happen Inn where we stopped for tea. He said he's got a nice young colt he wants to sell next spring after he's broken and schooled it. How would you like that?"

"Oh, Dad!" Trixie almost dropped the egg she was

holding. "Will he want an awful lot of money for his horse? Do you think I can earn enough by next summer?"

"I wouldn't be at all surprised," her father said, his eyes twinkling. "I'm delighted our new neighbors are being so generous with their horses and giving you a chance to learn to ride. Brian and Mart, of course, learned at camp. So I imagine that even if you didn't earn enough to buy the Tomlin colt yourself, you could interest your brothers in sharing in the purchase."

Trixie was so excited at the prospect of a horse on Crabapple Farm she could hardly eat her dinner, and it was a long time after she had gone to bed before she fell asleep. "I'll earn the money for the colt myself," she kept saying over and over. "He'll be as strong and fast as Jupiter, and although I'll let Brian and Mart ride him sometimes, he won't really like anyone but me."

Chapter 13
Understanding Regan

The next morning, Honey came down to the hollow right after breakfast. She was so excited that she burst right into the kitchen without knocking.

"Oh, I'm sorry," she cried, her cheeks aflame with embarrassment when she realized what she had done.

"Sorry for what?" demanded Trixie who was alone in the kitchen.

"For forgetting to knock," Honey explained. "I don't know what's come over me lately, Trixie." She giggled. "I seem to have forgotten all the good manners Miss Lefferts taught me."

"Pooh," Trixie said impatiently. "I don't know who Miss Lefferts is—or was, but I think you would have been awfully silly to knock when you could see me right through the screen door. People in the country don't bother much about knocking, anyway. We usually open the door, poke our heads inside and yell, 'Yoo-hoo.' "

Honey's giggle changed into loud laughter.

"What's so funny?" Trixie brought the breakfast cups to the sink and frowned at Honey.

"Oh, oh," Honey chortled. "If anybody did that in New York City—why—oh," she interrupted herself, still shaking with laughter, "you couldn't anyway. Not in the apartment house we lived in. Even if you managed to sneak by the doorman and the elevator boy, you couldn't open a door and poke your head inside. People in New York always keep their doors locked. At least people who lived in our apartment did."

"Sounds like prison," Trixie said, still frowning.

"It was, sort of," Honey admitted. "I mean, I used to ride up and down in the elevator day after day with the same people and they never spoke to me, even though we were neighbors, living on the same floor. Sometimes they would smile, but as for yelling 'Yoo-hoo'—" she went off into gales of laughter.

Trixie couldn't help laughing, too. Finally she sobered. "What you mean is that if we'd been neighbors in a big city we might never have met?"

Honey shook her head up and down. "And wouldn't that have been awful? Maybe not for you, but for me."

"For me, too," Trixie said emphatically. "I have lots of friends who live in Sleepyside, but I hardly ever see them during the summer. They seem to forget that I'm alive when school closes. And the funny thing is, Honey," she added frankly, "although I've known those

165

girls since we started in kindergarten together I don't like any of them half as much as I like you."

Honey gulped and looked as though she were going to go from laughter to tears. "I—I—you—you," she stammered, then quickly recovered her poise. "I just love you, and Jim, too. I wish you could have been with us yesterday on our ride. He's simply marvelous."

"I'll bet he is," Trixie said. "Tell me all about it while I wash these dishes."

"Let me help." Honey grabbed a dish towel off the rack and pulled a tall stool to the sink. "Oh, I forgot. Regan sent Bobby a present." She reached into the pocket of her jeans and brought out a small box. When she lifted the cover Trixie couldn't help letting out a little yell of surprise. The box was filled to the brim with tiny plastic horses—black ones and red ones and yellow ones. Some of them were trotting, some of them were galloping, and some of them were rearing with manes and tails flowing.

"I never saw anything so cute in my life," Trixie cried. "They must have cost a fortune! Bobby will adore them. It was darling of Regan to remember him."

"That's Regan for you," Honey said, carefully slipping the box back in her pocket. "He loves kids of all ages. One reason is because he didn't have a very happy childhood himself, I guess. He doesn't say much about it, but I couldn't help getting the impression that he had a pretty hard time while he was growing up."

"Maybe that's why he's so good to us, too," Trixie said as she handed Honey another plate.

Mrs. Belden appeared then with a trayful of dishes which she had just carried down from Bobby's room. "Good morning, Honey," she said. "I'm glad you dropped in. Wouldn't you like to run up and say hello to Bobby? It would cheer him up a lot. I've just given him a bath and dressed him in clean pajamas. He's ready for visitors."

"I'd love to," Honey said enthusiastically. "I have a present for him from Regan." She darted off.

Trixie took the tray from her mother and said, "I'll do these. Honey will help. She'll help with the gardening, too, I know. We won't leave until all the chores are done, Moms."

"Well, thank you, Trixie," Mrs. Belden said, sinking tiredly into the nearest chair. "Keeping Bobby quietly in bed is a fulltime job, but I want you to have fun, too. Do whatever you think is most important in the garden. Then you and Honey run along and forget about chores until lunchtime." She gathered up her knitting bag, some magazines and went back upstairs.

In another minute Honey joined Trixie in the

kitchen. "Bobby is *so* cute," she said enviously. "I'd give anything in the world for a little brother like that. And an older brother like Jim would be marvelous, too. He's really an expert horseman. He rides like a centaur. I mean, when he swings into the saddle it looks as though he and the horse were one. Jupiter behaved like a lamb yesterday—and you know Jupe."

"I certainly do," Trixie admitted ruefully. "I suppose Jim rode him with a snaffle bit and had him eating out of his hand."

"Well, not exactly," Honey said. "But Jim never had to use the curb. He talked to Jupe for a while before he mounted him, and they seemed to understand each other perfectly. Then we left the woods and rode across country through the fields, jumping fences and little brooks. It was the best ride I ever had. I wish you could have been with us."

"I don't know how to jump yet," Trixie reminded her. "So I couldn't have kept up with you. Am I going to have another lesson today?"

"This afternoon," Honey said. "And be careful when you talk to Regan. Even though I gave both horses a rubdown yesterday when I brought them back, I think Regan suspects something. Both saddle blankets were soaked with sweat, you know, and I couldn't do anything about that but let Regan think you and I had a short ride in the corral on Lady and Strawberry."

"I'll be careful," Trixie promised.

Honey helped her finish all the breakfast dishes, and then they went down to the garden. Trixie showed her how to hill up the potato vines, and, after an hour's work, they climbed the path to the Miser's Mansion.

"We're going to have one last look around," Trixie told Jim. "Why don't you take this flashlight and see what you can find in the cellar?"

Honey took the other flashlight and carefully inspected the shelves, cupboards, and closets while Trixie went through the stacks of books. "Mr. Frayne might have cut out the pages of one of them," she said, "and hid the money in there. Other people have done that."

They kept at it till lunchtime, and they were all completely discouraged. Jim washed up at the well and hungrily munched the cold turkey leg Trixie had brought him.

"There's just one other place," he said between mouthfuls. "The summerhouse. Now that I've got a flash-light, I can look in there for a trap door or something."

"That's right," Trixie encouraged him. "But I still have a feeling the money, or whatever it is, is in the living-room."

"Well, you're welcome to keep on searching through all that junk as long as you want to. I've given up. Either there isn't any money, or it's hidden too well for me to find it." He grinned. "I even went through that barrel of bottle tops this morning. What a mess that was!"

The girls went home for lunch then, and, after Trixie had read Bobby to sleep, she hurried up to the Wheelers' stable.

Regan said nothing about his suspicions during the lesson, but afterward, when the girls were helping him groom the horses, he said casually, "Thought that big old rambling house on the other hill was empty."

"It is," Trixie said quickly. "It belongs to old Mr. Frayne, and he's dying in the hospital."

"Huh." Regan pretended to be very busy with his curry-comb. "I've got a pretty good view of that place from my room over the garage," he said as though he were talking to himself. "Could have sworn I saw some-body roaming around there this morning. Matter of fact, was pretty sure that two of the three kids I saw were you girls."

Trixie and Honey stared at each other behind his back but said nothing. After a long, nerve-wracking silence, Regan began again. "Ran away from an orphanage myself when I was about that redheaded boy's age. Never regretted it, either. Was crazy over horses and finally got a job at a riding school. Learned a lot there," he went on reminiscently. "Learned enough, anyway, so I can tell right off whether a horse has been ridden or not." He straightened up to face them, his eyes twinkling. "Now Jupe here, he had a good gallop yesterday afternoon. Know neither one of you girls could have given him such a workout. Figure that redheaded kid knows how to handle a horse."

Trixie held her breath, not daring to look at Honey.

Regan gave Jupiter an affectionate slap. "I don't have much time to give you the proper amount of exercise with the boss away, do I, old boy? I'm not likely to say anything if Miss Honey, every now and then, takes you along when she goes off on Strawberry." He laughed. "Some people might think it peculiar that she bothers to saddle and bridle you when nobody's going to ride you, but me, I don't aim to ask any questions. There's just one thing, though. Trixie's got to promise to stick to Lady till I say the word. We'd all get into a lot of trouble if anything happened to Jupe." He placed his hands on his hips, grinning. "Is it a deal, girls?"

"Oh, yes," they both cried together.

"We'd like to tell you about it, Regan," Honey

171

added, "but we promised not to. I think you're simply swell to trust us."

"Well, that's that, then." Regan led Jupiter into his stall. "If the kid should get into any trouble, you might let me know. It wasn't so very long ago that I was hiding out in barns myself, wondering where the next meal was coming from."

He strolled nonchalantly out of the stable, and Trixie gasped, "Gee, he's great, isn't he, Honey? It was sure lucky nobody else in your house saw us. What a break!"

"Miss Trask's a good sport, too," Honey said loyally. "But I'm not sure what she'd do if she knew Jim had run away from home."

"She's swell," Trixie agreed. "But I bet she'd feel she ought to tell the police or try to talk Jim into going back."

"Let's surprise Jim by leading Jupe up to him tomorrow morning," Honey broke in. "We can ride through the bridle trails on the other side of Glen Road. Dad says it's a lovely ride, and if there are any gates we can open them for you, or you can ride around them."

"That would be wonderful," Trixie cried enthusiastically. "And sometime before Jim goes, let's go for a moonlight ride. The moon's almost full now, so it would be as light as day. Do you think Regan would let us?"

"I'm pretty sure he would," Honey said. "I have a feeling he must have seen Jim and me out riding yesterday afternoon. That's why he's so sure Jim can handle Jupiter. Regan went off in the Ford, you know, and he might have been driving along the back roads and seen us galloping through the fields beyond our property."

"Anyway," Trixie interrupted, "let's bring our lunches tomorrow and have a picnic in the woods. Dad said I deserved a day off, and the garden's practically free of weeds now, so I think Moms would let me go."

As Trixie waved good-by to Honey, she suddenly remembered that Mr. Lytell had said he was riding his old nag through the woods on the opposite side of the road when he saw smoke up at the Mansion. "Oh heck," she told herself. "That was *early* in the morning. By the time we start out, he'll be safely behind his counter in the store." She hurried along the path, because it was time to feed the chickens and she could see her father's car turning into the driveway. "And even if he should see Jim," she decided, "he won't know who he is. He couldn't possibly know everything!"

Chapter 14
A Night at the Manor House

Trixie scattered a handful of grain around the chicken-yard and was relieved to notice that the water can did not need refilling. Her father joined her as she gathered eggs.

"How many?" he asked.

"Only seven," she said.

"That's not too bad," he said. "The hens will start molting soon, and then we'll have to buy eggs until the pullets begin to lay." He pointed to a fat young cockerel that was greedily pecking the scratch. "He and his brother will make nice broilers for the weekend."

Trixie grinned. "Yummy-yum, but it doesn't seem possible that those baby chicks we bought in March are ready to eat. It seems like yesterday that they were nothing but balls of yellow fluff and Bobby and I made up our minds that we'd never, never eat anything so cute."

They strolled down the path to the terrace and Trixie asked, "How is Mr. Frayne, Dad? Did you stop at the hospital today?"

Mr. Belden shook his head. "No, but I telephoned

just before I left the bank. His condition is unchanged. I'm afraid the old gentleman hasn't a chance, Trixie. He was too undernourished, to begin with."

"I just don't understand it," Trixie said. "With all that money, you'd think he would have eaten a square meal occasionally."

"Nobody's sure that he did have any money," her father reminded her. "He may well have lost his entire fortune in bad investments, you know."

"How about the property?" Trixie asked. "It's worth a thousand dollars an acre, isn't it?"

"It may be heavily mortgaged," Mr. Belden said. "I'll inquire at the bank about that tomorrow. But even if it isn't mortgaged, Mr. Frayne may well have preferred starving to the risk of losing his land. A lot of people feel that way about their land, you know. They would rather die than sacrifice it."

Trixie thought of the closets on the top floor of the Mansion that were filled with expensive clothes which had been allowed to rot into shreds. The moth-eaten rugs, alone, could have been sold at one time for enough money to have kept the old man supplied with plenty of food for many months. *If he wouldn't sell anything in the house,* she reflected, *it stands to reason that he wouldn't part with a foot of his land. I'll bet Jim can count on a sure ten thousand dollars, anyway, when his uncle dies.*

"Tell me more about Mr. Frayne, Dad," she said, as they stretched out in two beach chairs on the terrace. "You know, what he was like before he got so queer."

"He and his wife were a charming old couple," her father told her. "They were so kind to us when we first moved up here that I can never forget it, no matter how unneighborly he became later. Your mother and I have always thought that if only he'd had children, he wouldn't have become such a complete recluse when his wife died. He was very fond of children—they both were—especially fond of little boys. Every time they went to the city they brought back presents for Brian and Mart. A big red express wagon one time, I remember. And when the boys had the chicken pox, both the Fraynes spent many hours every day reading stories to them, so your mother could get some rest."

"Why, they *were* nice, weren't they?" Trixie said in surprise. Suddenly she hoped that Mr. Frayne wouldn't die. If he lived, she felt sure that he would adopt Jim. *How wonderful that would be,* she thought excitedly. *And if Honey's parents would stay up here this winter, then we could all go to the same school and skate and ski together and everything!*

The whole prospect was so thrilling Trixie felt she

had to share her hopes with Honey. Right after supper she raced up the hill to the Manor House. Honey was still at the dinner table. She and Miss Trask were being served baked Alaska in the big formal dining-room. A maid brought another crystal dish for Trixie, but she was so awed by the gleaming silver and glass and the tall candles that she could hardly eat the delicious dessert.

"Maybe you'd like Honey to show you around the house," Miss Trask said when the maid brought in fingerbowls. "It's really a beautiful place; more of a showplace, right now, instead of a home. But we hope, with you and your brothers coming up here often, it'll get that lived-in feeling it needs."

"This is the library," Honey said, leading the way to a long room the walls of which were lined from floor to ceiling with richly bound books. "Daddy's quite a collector, you know. There was never enough space in our New York apartment for him to display all his books, so this is just about his favorite room."

"I never saw so many books in all my life," Trixie gasped. "He's got many more than there are in the village public library. You're lucky. You can do all your research work for school right here at home." And that reminded her of why she had come up to see Honey.

"Say," she went on, "do you think there's a chance of your staying up here all the year round? Did you speak to Miss Trask about it?"

Honey nodded. "Yes, and she said she'd do everything she could to persuade Mother to keep the house open. Even if Daddy and Mother spend most of the winter in town, Miss Trask hopes she and I can stay here, so I can go to school with you and your brothers."

"And Jim," Trixie interrupted. "Oh, I do hope Mr. Frayne lives and adopts him. We could all have such grand times together."

"I'm keeping my fingers crossed," Honey said as they passed through the library into the enormous living-room. "It looks like a museum, doesn't it?" she asked as Trixie stared about her at the luxurious furniture and priceless paintings. "And that's just what it is. Nobody ever comes in here except to *look*. I wish Daddy had bought a country place like yours." Tears welled up suddenly in her wide hazel eyes. "They moved up here just for my sake, but they never asked me where I wanted to live."

"Well, why didn't you come right out and tell them?" Trixie demanded impulsively. "Are you afraid of your parents, or something?"

Honey rubbed her eyes with clenched fists. "Not

exactly," she gulped. "Not of Daddy, anyway. He can be awfully sweet and sympathetic at times. But he's always so busy he's hardly ever at home, and when he is, Mother's always giving a party or dragging him out to one." She rubbed the toe of her shoe viciously into the thick pile of the heavy carpet. "I think Daddy would like living here if it weren't for Mother. She has to have people around her all the time. Not children, grownups. Mother doesn't like children, I guess."

"But she must like you," Trixie gasped. "Love you, I mean."

"I'm not so sure of that." Honey stared out of the window at the huge blue spruce tree which stood in front of the house. "She was awfully worried when I was so sick. She came right up to the infirmary herself when the school telephoned her. And she never left me until I was well enough to be taken home. But—But—" Honey suddenly crumpled into a little heap on the carpet and burst into tears. "But—I—still—don't think she loves me."

Trixie's own blue eyes filled with sympathy as she knelt beside Honey and tried to comfort her. "Of course she loves you," she kept saying over and over again, not knowing what else to say.

"No, she doesn't," Honey sobbed uncontrollably. "If

she did, why does she always send me away to schools and camps and have nurses and governesses take care of me instead of taking care of me herself the way other mothers do?"

"I don't know," Trixie admitted and then straightened as a sudden thought struck her. "You know what, Honey? Maybe she's afraid of you. Maybe she feels just as shy with you as you do with her. I think you ought to try talking more with her. What I mean is, you should tell her how you feel about things, instead of always going to Miss Trask. I'll bet my own mother would be awfully hurt if I told somebody else I wanted a bike or anything."

As though by magic, Honey's tears instantly stopped. She sat up and stared at Trixie. "Do you really think so?" she asked, flushing with excitement. "Do you think she'd listen when I told her—well, about my nightmares, for instance?"

"Of course, she'd listen," Trixie said firmly. "She's probably always wanted to be close to you but never knew how to begin."

Honey sprang to her feet. "I think you've got the answer, Trixie," she cried. "I remember now Daddy telling me a long time ago that Mother was very delicate when I was a baby. She still isn't terribly husky, and I guess I get my nervousness from her. I'll bet in the beginning she just wasn't strong enough to take care of me, and that's when the trouble began."

Trixie laughed with relief now that Honey was no longer in the dumps. "I'll bet your mother is exactly like you, Honey," she said. "You two will get on together like twin sisters once you get to know each other."

"I am supposed to look just like her," Honey admitted, pointing to a large portrait which hung on the far wall.

Trixie crossed over to look at it more closely. "Why, it's you twenty years from now," she giggled up at the lovely, slender-faced woman whose wide hazel eyes might have been Honey's. "What does your father look like?"

"I've got a big photograph of him in my room," Honey said. "Come on, let's go up there and get out of this morgue. This room always makes me weepy."

A maid was turning back the covers on Honey's bed as the girls came in. She unfolded a dainty, lace-trimmed nightgown and brought Honey's silk negligee and matching slippers from the closet. "Will you be wanting anything else tonight, Miss Honey?" she asked.

"No, thanks." Honey smiled and turned to Trixie. "Oh, I wish you could spend the night with me. We could have a long talk about everything and Celia would bring us breakfast in bed the next morning. Wouldn't you, Celia?"

The maid nodded. "Popovers and strawberry jam and one of cook's famous bacon omelets."

"Oh, please, Trixie," Honey begged. "If you do, we'll have an early start for our morning ride."

Trixie hesitated. The pale blue handkerchief-linen sheets and pillow cases on Honey's bed looked very inviting. And the idea of having breakfast in bed when she was perfectly well was such a novel one that she couldn't resist it. "I'll telephone Dad," she said. "If he'll let me off from feeding the chickens in the morning, I guess I can stay."

Mrs. Belden answered the phone when Trixie called and gave her permission to spend the night with Honey.

"May I have the whole day off, Moms?" Trixie asked. "We want to ride through the woods on the other side of the road and have a picnic lunch."

Her mother consulted Mr. Belden and came back with the word that Trixie deserved a day off. "Have a good time, dear," she said.

"Thanks, Moms, and good night." Trixie placed the phone back in its cradle and hurried down the long hall to Honey's room. "It's okay," she grinned. "I'll have to borrow something to sleep in. Haven't you anything else except those lacy nightgowns? I've slept in pajamas ever since I can remember."

"I've got pajamas." Honey pulled a long mirror away from the wall and revealed several rows of shelves. "These are my camp clothes," she said. "Take your pick. They're all too small for me now, but they ought to fit you even though you probably weigh more than I do."

The girls played Honey's radio while they showered and changed, and then Miss Trask came in to say it was time for them to turn out the lights.

"Don't talk too late," she cautioned as she left them alone. "At least, not loud enough for me to hear you," she finished with a laugh.

"She's really a great sport," Trixie whispered as she snuggled under the dainty sheet. "If I had to have a governess, I'd pick her every time."

"I love her," Honey confided. "You should have seen the one I had before Miss Trask came. She was Mother's secretary, too, because, of course, when I was away from home, there was nothing else for her to do. Mother liked her, but I couldn't stand her near me."

"What was the matter with her?" Trixie asked sleepily.

"Oh, everything." Honey sat bolt upright in bed. "I

can't sleep with all that moonlight pouring through the windows, but it's too hot to pull down the shades. Stay awake, Trixie, and I'll tell you about Miss Lefferts."

"Okay." Trixie suppressed a yawn and tried to prop her tired eyelids open. "What about Miss Lefferts?"

"Why, she was about six feet tall and she must have weighed two hundred pounds." Honey giggled. "And yet she never made a sound when she walked. She was always sneaking up behind me and asking me if I'd done my piano lessons or embroidering or letter writing. She almost drove me crazy. She was the one who bought all those silly clothes in my closets and bureau drawers. She simply couldn't resist anything with lace and ruffles on it. Wouldn't she have a fit if she saw me in dungarees?"

"She sounds like something out of a book," Trixie said, between a yawn and a laugh. "I'll have a nightmare myself if you keep on talking about her. How did you happen to get rid of her?"

"That's the funny part of it," Honey said thoughtfully. "And I guess it proves you're right about me and my mother. When they brought me home from the school infirmary, there was Miss Lefferts waiting for me, armed to the teeth with all sorts of deadly dull projects which I could do in bed. I took one look at her and burst into tears."

"I should think you would have," Trixie said sympathetically. "Then what?"

"Why, then," Honey went on, "Daddy and Mother got awfully upset and asked me what was the matter. I couldn't stop crying, but finally I began to talk about Miss Trask and how much I liked her. She was the math instructor at school, and we got to be friendly, because I'm not very good at algebra and needed special tutoring. She told me how she had to support an invalid sister, and I knew Daddy paid Miss Lefferts much more than the school paid Miss Trask. Anyway, I never saw Miss Lefferts again, and when school closed at the end of May, Miss Trask arrived to be my new governess. I think she's just perfect!"

Honey was silent for a while after that, and Trixie was just dozing off when she heard a strange, scratching sound at the door. She leaned on her elbow and saw that Honey was sound asleep. In spite of herself, Trixie felt little shivers run up and down her spine. There were so many big, empty rooms in the house, and, except for the scratching, it was as quiet as a tomb.

Trixie suddenly felt homesick. She had never spent the night away from her family before in all her life, and she wished now that she were in her own bed across the hall from Bobby. The scratching continued, and then she heard a little, snuffling whine on the other side of the door.

It must be Honey's little cocker puppy, she thought with relief as she scrambled out of bed to let Buddy in. The puppy wriggled with joy when she opened the door, and Trixie scooped him up into her arms. "Were you lonely, too, Bud?" she crooned, nestling him against her pajama top.

Honey woke up, then. "Oh, I forgot to let Buddy in," she cried. "I'm sorry he woke you up. He always sleeps on the rug by my bed."

The puppy jumped out of Trixie's arms to lick Honey's face, then curled up happily beside her. In a few minutes, both girls were sound asleep. When Trixie opened her eyes again, sunlight was flooding the room, and Celia was standing in the doorway with a tray heaped high with two delicious breakfasts.

Chapter 15
Mr. Lytell's Curiosity

Jim stared at them in amazement when the girls appeared at the Mansion after breakfast, leading Jupiter.

"Regan knows all about you," Honey said, answering the question in his eyes. "We didn't tell. He saw us yesterday morning from his room over the garage."

Jim's broad shoulders slumped. "Then that does it. He'll tell the police, of course."

"Oh, no, he won't," Trixie put in. "He won't tell anybody, Jim. And he wants you to ride Jupe. He said so."

Jim looked worried but he grinned. "Regan must be some guy!" He swung up on the back of the big black gelding, and as Jupiter began to prance, anxious to be off, the worried expression on Jim's face faded into one of sheer delight. "I guess I'll risk it," he said. "I won't be around much longer, anyway. What have we here?" He pointed to the saddle bags in which Honey had packed the lunch.

"Sandwiches and cake and milk." Honey smiled. "We're going to ride through the trails on the other side of Glen Road and have a picnic in the woods."

"Swell." Jim's legs were almost as long as Regan's, so he pulled up the stirrup leather only one notch. He was an expert horseman, Trixie could see at once, and, no matter how much Jupiter reared and danced, Jim never moved an inch from the saddle. "You make me think of a centaur," she said. "You sort of blend right into that horse."

Jim's green eyes sparkled. "What I wouldn't give to own this fellow! And I bet I could get his mouth in shape in a couple of weeks. The fellow who schooled Jupe probably used a spade bit on him, that's why he fights the bit so now. With a little gentle handling, he'd respond to a snaffle in no time."

"Dad's got awfully heavy hands," Honey admitted. "He loves horses and is one of the best riders in the Squadron, but he hasn't much patience. He loses his temper very quickly. Sometimes he scares me." She led the way down the rutted road from the Mansion. "He's like Regan, though. He gets mad and gets over it so fast it sort of leaves you breathless."

"That's the kind of guy I like," Jim said, as he forced Jupiter to walk down behind Lady. "Jonesy is just the opposite. He broods a lot, and it takes him a long time to work himself up into a rage, and when he does, he goes almost insane. If he beat me in a moment of anger, I wouldn't mind it so much. Then it would be over and done with quickly. I can tell in the morning when he's mad about something, and it smolders in him all day long, and I go around waiting for the moment when he's going to grab me and drag me out to the barn." He chuckled. "He's working himself up into a lather now, I bet. He'd half kill me if he ever caught me."

Trixie shuddered inwardly. "That must never happen," she told herself. "Never, never."

At the foot of the hill, Jim reined in Jupiter behind a clump of bushes while the girls made sure that nobody was in sight. Jupiter reared impatiently. When they had safely crossed Glen Road, Jim let him out. The big horse pounded along the trail, well in the lead, and when Jim thought Jupe had had enough of a run, he stopped and waited for Trixie and Honey to catch up. Foam dripped from the horse's mouth as he worried the bit. Jim patted his neck soothingly.

"There, there, boy. They've got you all strapped up in a martingale so you can't rear as high as you'd like, haven't they? If you were mine," Jim said, half to himself, half aloud, "I'd let you rear your head off. I know what it's like to be tied up. The first time I ran away, Jonesy caught me and tied me, hand and foot, to the bed for three days. I thought I'd go crazy."

"Oh," Honey gasped. "How awful! How did you ever have the nerve to run away again?"

Jim shrugged. "It wasn't so much nerve as it was sheer desperation. And the straw that broke the camel's back was the way he jeered when I told him I'd won a scholarship to college. I'd made up my mind, you see, to stick it out for another year, because, once I got into college, the worst would be over. I worked like anything to do two years in one and still keep at the head of the class." He grinned. "And I don't like to study much, either. Geometry practically threw me, but it was like a game. Anything to get away from Jonesy. And then, when everything was all set, he announced that he wasn't going to let me go to college. Said it would be a waste of time, because I'd flunk out the first year. Gosh, it was all I could do to keep from socking him."

"I don't see why you didn't," Trixie cried impulsively. "I bet you could beat him up."

Jim laughed. "I don't know about that. Jonesy's a powerful man, even though he's so stoop-shouldered he isn't much taller than I am. But, anyway, you don't go around socking older people. You just beat it."

"Whatever do you suppose made him such a beast?" Honey wondered. "He sounds crazy to me."

"He is crazy," Jim told her. "Crazy about money. You

191

might think Uncle James was a miser, Trixie, but you don't know Jonesy. He's kept books on how much it's cost him ever since I went to live with him. He put down every penny he gave me for a pad or pencil, even postage stamps, and he watched every mouthful of food I ate, weighing and measuring it."

"Golly," Trixie breathed. "Did he starve you, too, Jim?"

"No, he didn't do that," Jim said. "I was like an animal that had to be kept well-fed so it could work hard. He always had me checked by a doctor regularly, and he saw to it that I had good shoes and warm clothing. If he hadn't, the neighbors would have reported him to the police. But they know about the beatings. One of them interfered once, and Jonesy was so scared he didn't touch me for several days after that. He's smart. If the neighbors complained, another guardian might be appointed, and Jonesy would lose control of Uncle James's money. Not that I think there is any."

"Ten thousand dollars is a lot of money," Trixie insisted. "It would see you through college, anyway."

"*If* the place isn't mortgaged," Jim reminded her. "And if Uncle James didn't make another will. Anyway, Jonesy can have it. I guess I've cost him that much in the last five years."

They cantered along silently for a while, and when they came to a gate Jim and Honey sailed over it.

"Oh, please, let me try it," Trixie begged. "I know I can do it! I know I can."

Jim reached over to unhook the rope which held the wooden bars in place. "No, sir," he said firmly. "We're not going to do anything to get Regan mad at us. All you need is a broken collarbone to make everything just dandy."

Trixie bit her lip as the gate swung open and Lady walked through. "It looks so easy," she complained.

"Well, it's not," Jim told her. "There's a trick to jumping. If you got panicky and pulled on the reins instead of giving the horse his head, you could have a nasty accident. Also, Lady would sense that you're a beginner, and she might refuse at the last minute. You'd go sailing over her head, which wouldn't be any fun." He smiled at Trixie's flushed face. "Take it easy, kid. Start with a foot-high hurdle and work up. There's no sense in getting a lot of broken ribs unless you have to."

Trixie knew he was right, so she walked meekly around the next barrier without a word. When the sun was high in the sky they stopped for lunch beside a shallow stream. The horses drank thirstily and grazed quietly in the shade, even Jupiter being grateful for a chance to rest and cool off.

"It's at moments like this," Jim said, stretching out on the soft pine needles under the branches of the huge evergreens, "that I forget all about Jonesy. It's the nights I hate. The floors in that old house groan and creak all night long, and I keep waking up expecting to find Jonesy standing over me with a whip in his hands."

"I hate the nights, too," Honey said sympathetically. "And I don't see how you can stay in that eerie place all alone. I bet it's full of rats."

"Mice," Jim said, "but I don't mind them. They're kind of friendly, and one of them's practically tame, so he must have been Uncle James's pet. By the way, you haven't heard anything more about my uncle, have you?"

Trixie shook her head. "No, but Dad's going to stop at the hospital sometime today, so I'll have news this evening." She rolled over and sat up. "We really ought to be starting back. I haven't the faintest idea where we are. Has anybody else?"

"Not me," Honey admitted. "But then, I have absolutely no sense of direction."

Jim held up his hand warningly. "Somebody's riding along the trail." He leaped on Jupiter's back. "I'd better hide behind those bushes on the other side of the brook."

When Jupiter and Jim had disappeared, Honey

edged Strawberry closer to Lady. "I'm scared," she said. "Maybe we're trespassing."

"I think this land belongs to the State," Trixie whispered back, "but I'm not sure." And then the horse and rider came around the bend in the trail. "It's Mr. Lytell," Trixie breathed. "Golly, I forgot the store is closed on Tuesdays on account of being open Sundays."

Mr. Lytell was riding a gray, sway-backed mare with gaunt hipbones and discouraged-looking eyes. She stumbled to a stop beside Lady and immediately hung her head, almost as if she knew the other horses were making fun of her.

"Hello, girls," Mr. Lytell greeted. "Had a picnic, I see."

"We just finished," Honey said. "It's a lovely day, isn't it?"

"Too hot for my Belle," he said, patting the gray's neck. "Pretty far from home, aren't you?"

"I don't know," Trixie said. "Are we?"

He poked at his glasses. "Lost, huh? Well, just follow me, and I'll show you the way back."

"Oh, no, thanks," Trixie said hastily. "We're not ready to go home yet."

"Just as you say." He picked up the reins, and Belle obediently stumbled forward. "But this trail is like a maze. It goes round and round, crossing and recrossing itself. You could be lost for hours if you're not familiar with the landmarks." He waved to them with his crop. "We may meet up again."

"I hope we don't," Trixie said under her breath as he disappeared through the trees. She whistled and Jim came riding back across the brook.

"It was Mr. Lytell," Trixie said. "We've got to be careful. He knows everybody for miles around, and he doesn't miss a thing that goes on. He's a regular old gossip."

"What direction did he take?" Jim asked.

"The same way we came."

"Then we'd better take this fork," Jim said. "I'm taking no chances. Sooner or later, Jonesy'll come snooping around here, and it would be too bad if Mr. Lytell was able to describe me." He nudged Jupiter into a canter. "That's the trouble with having red hair. Nobody ever misses it."

They rode along single file for about twenty minutes and stopped when they came to another fork in the bridle trail. "I don't know which way to go now," Jim said. "Any ideas, Trixie?"

Trixie shook her head. "As far as I'm concerned, we've been lost for hours. I've never been this far into these woods."

"If we could see the river," Jim said thoughtfully, "I'd know what to do. But we're so far down in the valley I doubt if I could see it even if I climbed a tree." He squinted up at the sky. "Well, the sun's beginning to set, so that way's west. We want to go north so let's take this fork and see what happens."

An hour passed, and Trixie began to realize that she was not as experienced a rider as the others. Her back ached, and her legs felt numb and stiff. "Golly," she groaned, "I'm so tired I could fall out of the saddle and go right to sleep on the ground. How near are we to home, Jim?"

Jim frowned. "This is a regular labyrinth! The trail goes round and round in circles. We haven't been getting anywhere since we took that right-hand fork."

"Well, here's the brook," cried Honey, who was in the lead. "Maybe if we follow it, we'll get back to where we had lunch." She turned around in the saddle. "This looks sort of famil—"

At that moment, Strawberry placed his foot in a hole and stumbled. Before Honey could turn back and gather up the reins, the horse went down on his knees, so violently that Honey pitched over his head. Strawberry quickly scrambled to his feet and, finding himself riderless, set off at a run with Jim, on Jupiter, after him. Trixie slid off Lady's back and hurried to help Honey to her feet.

"I'm all right," Honey said. "It was dumb of me to let the reins get so slack. If I hadn't been careless, I could have pulled Strawberry up before he stumbled so badly."

"I'm glad to know that even good riders fall off, sometimes," Trixie said, grinning.

Honey rubbed her ankle. "Trixie, I hope Jim catches Strawberry. We're probably miles from home."

It seemed like hours that they waited, and the sun got so low in the sky that it was twilight under the heavy branches of the evergreens. "I'm too tired to move," Trixie said, at last, "but I think we'd better start back. Jim's probably lost us by now."

They started off, leading Lady between them, and then Trixie noticed that Honey was limping. "Honey," she cried. "You've hurt yourself. Let me see your leg."

Honey rolled up her blue jeans, and Trixie saw that her ankle was swelling above her shoe. "It's nothing," Honey said. "Just a wrench. I can manage."

"It must hurt like the dickens," Trixie said. "You get up on Lady. You shouldn't walk on it until it's strapped. Dad can do it for you when we get home."

"If we ever get home." Honey giggled. "I feel like an

awful dope sitting up here with you walking. It was my horse that ran away, not yours."

"They're both your horses," Trixie reminded her, with a laugh. "Anyway, I feel so stiff and sore I don't think I could climb into a saddle."

"Well, here comes somebody," Honey said, listening to hoofbeats just ahead of them. "I wouldn't even mind if it was Mr. Lytell at this point. I'd hate to spend the night in these woods."

And then they saw that it was Jim on Jupiter, leading Strawberry. "I had to circle around to head him off," he explained. "That's what took so long. As it was, I didn't catch him until he was just a few yards from Glen Road. Anyway," he finished, "Strawberry showed me the way back."

"Honey twisted her ankle when she fell," Trixie told Jim. "I'll ride Strawberry back."

"Oh, no, you won't." Honey slid out of the saddle, wincing as her ankle touched the ground. "Remember our promise to Regan."

"I forgot," Trixie admitted as Jim helped Honey mount Strawberry. "Oh, quick, Jim, somebody's coming."

But it was too late for Jim to hide, and in a minute Mr. Lytell appeared on a narrow path off the main trail.

"So we meet again," he said, staring curiously at

Jim. "That's a beautiful horse. I think I saw your father riding him early Friday morning."

A dull red crept up Jim's cheeks to his ears, and Trixie could guess how he hated acting a lie.

Honey said with quick tact, "Dad *was* out on Jupiter Friday, Mr. Lytell. He went to Canada Saturday night. Mother can't stand this heat, you know."

"I can't stand it myself." Mr. Lytell began polishing his glasses. "The perspiration fogs up my specs so I can't see." He peered nearsightedly at Jim. "You don't look much like your sister, do you?"

"We don't look at all alike," Honey said truthfully, and Trixie felt nervous laughter bubbling up inside her. Jim's face was almost as red as his hair as he silently swung up on Jupiter. "We'd better start for home," he mumbled uncomfortably.

"Yes, indeed," Mr. Lytell nudged Belle into a walk. "It's time for me to go to the train for the city papers. I'm taking the short cut to the store, but you youngsters had better stick to the trail."

They watched him move slowly through the trees, and Trixie sighed with relief. "Whew! He's so nosy. Honey, you were wonderful to let him go on thinking Jim was your brother."

Jim's jaw was set. "And this is just the beginning,"

he thought out loud, his green eyes dark with misery. "It'll be one lie after another, I guess, if I don't want to get caught." He slumped in the saddle. "I don't think I can stand it."

Trixie felt a quick pang of sympathy. She hated to lie herself and remembered how miserable she always felt whenever she evaded the truth. "You didn't really lie, Jim," she tried to comfort him. "And neither did Honey. That nosy old man had no business prying in your business, anyway."

Jim straightened. "Well, I'm not going to lie when I apply for a job as a junior counselor. I couldn't live with myself if I did."

"But," Honey objected, "they won't hire you if they find out you ran away from home, will they?"

"That remains to be seen." Jim shrugged. "I'm strong, and I'm good with animals. They'll give me a job on a cattle boat without asking any questions. I'd like to see Europe, anyway."

They rode back to the Mansion in a depressed silence.

"Thanks a lot," Jim said as he handed Jupiter's reins to Honey. "If I shouldn't see you again, I want you to know how much I appreciate all you two did for me."

"Now, Jim." Honey's huge hazel eyes clouded with

tears. "Promise you won't go away without first letting us know."

"I can't promise anything," he said almost brusquely and vaulted in through the window.

Regan was waiting for the girls at the stable. "You've been gone a lot longer than you thought you would," he said, trying to hide his anxiety. "Have any trouble?"

Honey told him about her fall, and Regan carefully examined her ankle. "I'll strap that up for you, so it won't bother you at all." He glanced out of one eye at Trixie. "You look all in," he told her. "I'll give Lady her rubdown. Run along home, now."

"Thanks," Trixie murmured and went wearily down the road.

Trixie was so tired she didn't see how she was going to make herself feed the chickens, but somehow she managed to throw out the grain and gather the eggs. As she came out of the coop, she saw her father putting his car away in the garage. "Any news of Mr. Frayne, Dad?" she called out.

Mr. Belden closed the doors to the garage before replying. "Yes," he said soberly. "He died this afternoon."

Chapter 16
Unwelcome Guests

"Oh, Dad." Trixie looked up at the Mansion, thinking, *Poor Jim! He's alone in the world, now. Even if Mr. Frayne was a mean old miser, at least he was somebody Jim felt he belonged to.* Aloud she asked her father, "Did he say anything before he died? About a will, I mean."

"No." Mr. Belden looked grave. "He never regained consciousness. We're still trying to locate some member of his family, but so far without success. There was a nephew, I remember; but he died about five years ago, and nobody knows what became of his widow." He walked slowly beside Trixie to the house. "It's too bad, because there's no mortgage on that property and it's worth at least ten thousand dollars. The widow and her children, if there are any, would inherit it."

"Where are they looking for her, Dad?" Trixie asked.

"Mainly in Rochester, where she was living at the time of her husband's death; but, so far, all the Fraynes we've contacted in New York state do not belong to the same family."

It was on the tip of Trixie's tongue to suggest that maybe the widow had married again, but she thought better of it and said nothing. Such a trail would lead straight to Jonesy, which was the one thing Jim wanted to avoid.

Trixie did her chores early the next morning and raced up the hill to bring Jim the latest news.

"He's dead, Jim," she said quietly. "I'm awfully sorry. I wish there was something I could do."

Jim stared down at the toe of his moccasin.

"They're trying to find your mother," Trixie said uncomfortably.

"Then that settles it," Jim said. "Sooner or later, Jonesy will appear on the scene. I'd better be on my way now."

"Jim, please." Trixie thought she couldn't stand it if Jim went off by himself. "It's all so unfair. This place belongs to you now, and there's no reason why you shouldn't have the money from the sale of it." She stopped as a heavy droning sound filled the air, and, looking up, she saw a squadron of airplanes approaching from the north.

As they stared up at the sky, one of the planes dropped out of formation and began flying very low. "Looks like it's going to land somewhere," Jim said.

"Golly, it's turning over and over! That doesn't look like a stunt to me! Wonder if the pilot's having trouble?"

As he spoke, there was the deafening sound of an explosion and the plane burst into flames. It hurtled through the air, careening dangerously close to the Wheelers' house; then, shooting flames and roaring like a dozen fire engines, it crashed into the woods on the other side of Glen Road.

Trixie was so horrified that she didn't realize that she had clutched Jim's arm and was yelling at the top of her lungs. Then she saw something white up in the sky and realized, with relief, that the pilot had bailed out before the plane exploded.

"The wind's blowing in this direction," Jim said. "He's bound to come down somewhere near here."

Already, the parachute was floating just above the trees on the wooded hill, and in a minute it passed over their heads so close to where they were standing that they could see the tense face of the young pilot. Then the folds of the 'chute became entangled in the branches of a tall tree on the east side of the Mansion. Jim and Trixie raced across the clearing and through the field. The pilot was perched on a branch of the tree, unbuckling his 'chute.

Trixie gazed up at him. "Are you hurt?" she called breathlessly.

His face was pale, but he grinned as he climbed to the ground. "No, but, boy, oh, boy, I thought I was going to be. I don't know what happened to that engine, but I bailed out just in time." He leaned weakly against the tree trunk. "I am a little shaky. Where am I, anyway?"

"You're on the Frayne place," Trixie told him. "I'm Trixie Belden, and I live down in the hollow. This is—" She turned around to introduce Jim. "Why, he's gone."

"The redheaded kid?" The young lieutenant pulled off his helmet and mopped his face. "He disappeared in those bushes over there. Maybe he doesn't like pilots." He laughed. "But a lot of others seem to be interested." He pointed down to the road.

As if by magic, Glen Road had suddenly become packed with cars and trucks, and people were already swarming up the rutted driveway. Two policemen reached the clearing first and began questioning the pilot, while Trixie ran around to the back of the house to bring him a drink of water. When she returned from the well, reporters were scribbling in their notebooks, and a news photographer was taking a picture of the pilot with the old Mansion in the background. Then she saw Mr. Lytell climbing up the short cut from the hollow, though how he got there so quickly Trixie didn't know. Regan and Honey came galloping through the woods on horseback, and in a few minutes the clearing was filled with a crowd of milling, curious people.

"The ground shook for miles around when that plane crashed," Mr. Lytell was telling the pilot. "You were lucky to get out in time."

"Say, I've got to call headquarters and report," the lieutenant interrupted. "Is there a phone in this old house?"

"Not here," Mr. Lytell said. "This is the Frayne place. He was an eccentric old man. Supposed to be a miser. Died yesterday of pneumonia, I hear."

"A miser?" The reporters moved closer to the house and peered in through the windows. "Zowie!" one of them yelled. "Look at all that junk. This'll make a swell yarn."

"Take all the pictures you want of the outside," a policeman cautioned. "But don't any of you cross the threshold without a permit from the chief. Come on," he said to the pilot. "Our car's parked down below. We'll drive you in to the station and you can make your report from there."

"Oh, no," Honey whispered to Trixie. "All these people! And look at that photographer. He's taking pictures of the living-room through the open window. Where's Jim?"

"I don't know," Trixie whispered back. "He just disappeared suddenly."

Regan cantered away, leading Strawberry, and in a short while the crowd dwindled down to Mr. Lytell and the girls.

"Lucky we weren't in those woods today," he said, shaking his head. "The fire department was having quite a time down there when I drove past."

Trixie and Honey stared down at the wisp of smoke that was rising above the pine trees. "Golly," Trixie breathed. "Do you suppose they'll be able to put it out?"

"Oh yes," Mr. Lytell said. "There wasn't enough left of the plane by the time it hit the ground to start much of a fire. Never saw anything like that before in all my life. The explosion was deafening down at the store. Even Belle was startled, and she's stone deaf." He chuckled. "And where did all those cars come from? I couldn't park any nearer than the Wheeler place. The plane had hardly hit the ground before there was a solid line from here to the Post Road." He peered through his glasses at Honey. "Funny your brother wasn't up here, too. Strikes me that a boy his age would be kind of interested in a pilot bailing out of an exploding plane."

"My little brother got bitten by a copperhead," Trixie said hastily. "You know, Bobby."

"Read about it in the paper," Mr. Lytell said. "Glad to hear he's doing so well." He moved over to the open window. "Better close this. It might rain, although it doesn't look like it. Those nosy reporters must have left it open."

Trixie thought he would never go away, but finally he did and she whistled, "Bob *White!* Bob *White!*"

Jim came crawling out from the old arbor that led to the summerhouse. "Whew!" he said. "Some excitement. The story will bc in the New York papers for sure. I don't dare hang around here any longer."

"No, Jim," Trixie broke in. "I've got a plan. Dad and Mother are leaving right after lunch for the seashore. The doctor thought the change would be good for Bobby." She turned to Honey. "I was going to ask you the first chance I got. They said I could stay home if you stayed with me. Just for the night. Dad'll be back tomorrow. Do you think Miss Trask'll let you?"

"I guess so," Honey said. "But why don't you spend the night with me, instead?"

Trixie shook her head. "No, it's better this way, because our house is nearer the Mansion. As soon as the family leaves, Jim can hide down there, and you and I

211

can give the place one last search. Please, Jim," she finished. "One more day. You'll be perfectly safe in our house, and there's going to be a full moon tonight, so maybe we could go for a moonlight ride."

"Well, all right," Jim said, after thinking it over for a minute. "But I'd better hit the road the first thing in the morning."

When Trixie got home, Bobby was full of the story of the plane crash. "Our house shook so I almost fell out of bed," he told Trixie. "Mummy said the pilot came down up at the Mansion. Did you see him? Did he get hurt?"

"Yes, I saw him," Trixie said. "And he wasn't hurt at all. But the plane was blown to bits."

Bobby bounced up and down in bed. "It 'sploded in midair," he yelled. "Hey! Soon's I get well I'm going to 'splore through those woods for shiny pieces of metal. You're not the only one who can 'splore 'round here."

Mrs. Belden came in with Bobby's luncheon tray. "It was certainly thrilling," she said. "I was down in the garden picking lettuce, and it looked to me as though the plane missed the Wheelers' chimney by inches." She tied a napkin under Bobby's chin. "Is Honey going to stay with you, Trixie? If not, you'd better start packing. I'm not at all sure we ought to leave you girls here alone, but your father seems to think you'll be perfectly all right."

"Of course we will," Trixie said quickly. "And it's only for one night."

Her mother snapped the lock on a small suitcase. "Bobby and I will probably stay for a week or ten days. The doctor said he could play quietly on the beach tomorrow and go in swimming by the weekend." She pinched Bobby's pale cheek. "You've got to get back those big red apples, you know."

"Don't worry about anything while you're gone," Trixie said. "I'll take good care of Dad. It'll be fun cooking for him."

She waved good-by to the family from the terrace, and in a little while she heard a bobwhite call from the woods behind the garage. She whistled back, and in a moment Jim darted out and ran down the driveway with Reddy barking at his heels.

"Saw the car leaving," he said. "I don't even feel safe here. Mind if I go in?"

"Of course not." Trixie led him into the living-room. "You don't have to worry. Nobody'll arrive without warning. Reddy barks his head off at everybody."

"That's pretty good." Jim stared around the low-ceilinged room admiringly. "This is a nice place. It reminds me of the house we had in the country before

Dad got sick. We had to sell it then and move to a small apartment in Rochester." His eye fell on a loving cup on the mantel. "Golly, I left in such a hurry I forgot to bring down my cup and the will."

"Honey and I'll bring them down this afternoon, after we search. Can I fix you some lunch now?" Trixie asked.

Jim shook his head. "I've already eaten, but I would like a hot shower. It was awfully hard keeping clean up there. I washed my shirt and pants a couple of times, but I couldn't really get the dirt out in that cold water."

"You can have all the hot water and soap you want," Trixie said. "And I'll find you some of Brian's clothes. While you're in the shower, I'll wash the ones you have on. They'll dry in no time in this hot sun."

Honey came down around four o'clock, and the girls bicycled to the store for the New York evening papers.

"They just arrived," Mr. Lytell told them, pointing to the first page.

Pilot Bails Out At Miser's Mansion the headline read, and in the bank under it were the words, *Missing Heiress Sought in Rochester.*

"Isn't that just like a newspaper?" Honey giggled. "They would make it a girl!" She clapped her hand over her mouth as Trixie's elbow dug into her ribs. But it was too late.

Mr. Lytell glanced at her with quick suspicion. "Eh, what's that?" he started to say.

Trixie grabbed the paper. On page two were pictures of the Mansion and the debris-filled living-room. Trixie read the caption out loud: "In this house and perhaps in this very room a fortune may be hidden."

"I doubt that." Mr. Lytell walked with the girls as far as the door. "In my opinion, Mr. Frayne died a pauper. What was that you were saying about a girl?"

"Nothing," Trixie said hastily. They got on their bikes and pedaled away from the store. "Oh," she moaned, "Jim isn't going to like this at all. I wish we didn't have to show him the papers." Then she added, "You must be more careful, Honey!"

"I know it," Honey said shamefacedly. "I almost let the cat out of the bag, and that man's suspicious enough anyway."

Chapter 17
Treasure

The freckles stood out in the whiteness of Jim's face as he read the newspaper account of the plane crash. The first two paragraphs covered the pilot's story, but the rest of the report was concerned with Mr. Frayne's recent death and the fact that there was no way of tracing the niece-in-law who would inherit the estate.

A reply to a query in Albany, just received, the story ended, *revealed a birth certificate for a boy, James Winthrop Frayne II, who, if he is still alive, would be fifteen years old this month. Authorities are making every effort to locate this boy and his mother who seem to have vanished into thin air after the death of the boy's father, five years ago.*

"We didn't vanish," Jim said, staring at the newsprint. "We stayed right on in Rochester until Mother married Jonesy. Then we went to live on his farm outside of Albany." He turned the page to the photograph of the miser's cluttered living-room. "What a bad break," he said slowly. "That christening mug of mine which I left on the mantelpiece stands out more clearly than anything else in the room. The light must have hit it. If Jonesy sees this particular picture, he'll know just where to look for me. I'd better get going."

"You can't," Honey wailed. "Everything's all set for tonight. Regan said we could go for a moonlight ride at nine o'clock if you went with us. He's going to have the horses ready. All three of them, Jim," she pleaded. "Don't you want to have one last ride on Jupe?"

Jim was obviously tempted. He ran his hand nervously through his thick red hair. "Gosh, I'd like to," he admitted, at last. "And even if Jonesy does see this picture, he isn't apt to come around here until tomorrow sometime."

Trixie let out a sigh of relief. "Come on, Honey," she said, starting for the screen door to the terrace. "If Jim's really going to leave the first thing in the morning, we'd better start right now giving the Mansion one last thorough search."

"I think you're wasting your time," Jim said. "But go ahead. I'll read this book I found. And please don't forget to bring back my mug and the Bible."

"I think we're wasting our time, too," Honey said as she and Trixie climbed up the hill with Reddy racing ahead of them. "And if we don't find anything, I want to give Jim some money before he goes, Trixie. I never spend my allowance, you know, and I'd like him to have it. But I don't quite dare. He might be insulted."

"I thought about that, too," Trixie said. "I've got five dollars coming to me at the end of the week and I almost asked Dad for it today, so I could give it to Jim. But I doubt if he'd accept it. He's awfully proud and stubborn."

"I know," Honey agreed. "I wouldn't like him if he were any different, but just the same I wish he'd let us help him."

Trixie clambered over the window sill. "The best way to help him is to find his uncle's money. Why don't you tap around that desk in the study, and see if you can find a secret panel while I work in the living-room. I'm still sure it's hidden in there somewhere."

Trixie felt along the paneled walls of the living-room, but without success. "There's no sense in going through those books and papers again," she told herself. "And we've moved everything at least twice looking for a trap door. I'd better give up in here and try the dining-room."

Honey joined her then, and together they pulled away the heavy mahogany sideboard. Dust was caked inches high on the baseboard behind it, and the wallpaper was streaked with grease and dirt.

"There's no secret hiding place here," Honey said after a while. "But how about that big picture on the other wall? In books, there's always a wall safe behind an old family portrait."

"Well, that's not a portrait," Trixie said, with a giggle. "It's just about the ugliest still life I ever saw. Look at those hideous flowers and that stiff bowl of fruit. That apple," she said giving it an exasperated poke, "is no more an apple than I am a—" She stopped in surprise, for suddenly the whole picture frame sprang away from the wall revealing a hidden alcove. "Honey," she cried, "I must have accidentally pressed the button which releases a spring. I thought that apple looked as though it had been painted in as an afterthought." She ran into the other room for her flashlight.

"Empty," Honey moaned. "Absolutely empty. Did you ever know anything like it? That old miser must have—"

"Wait a minute," Trixie interrupted. "There *is* something way back in the corner." She thrust her hand into the alcove and triumphantly pulled out a tiny, leather-covered jewel case. With a flick of her fingernail she snapped open the gold clasp. "It's an old-fashioned engagement ring," she gasped. "Golly, did you ever see such an enormous diamond?"

"It's huge," Honey breathed excitedly. "And it must

have belonged to Jim's great-aunt. Now I know his uncle was crazy. He hid her ring in here, boarded up the top floors, and deliberately let the summerhouse and the arbor get overgrown. It just doesn't make sense. I'll bet he did lose all his money in bad investments."

"I'm not so sure of that," Trixie said slowly. "It does make some sense, you know. He just didn't want anything around to remind him of his wife. Anyway, this ring is probably worth a lot of money, and I'm glad we found it for Jim." She stopped. "Oh, heck, somebody's coming. I can hear Reddy barking."

Together the girls crept to the open window and saw Reddy racing in angry, threatening circles around a man who had a camera strapped to one shoulder.

"It's another newspaper photographer," Trixie whispered. "Boy, I hope Reddy scares him away."

"I heard the policeman tell them not to go inside the house," Honey whispered back. "He won't dare come in, will he, Trixie?"

"That man wasn't here this morning," Trixie told her. "He's probably from the city. Oh, gosh, he's not the least bit afraid of Reddy. Look, he's patting his head, and Reddy's eating it up."

"We'd better hide somewhere," Honey said, in a frightened voice. "Oh, where'll we go, Trixie?"

"In the cellar," Trixie hissed. "Quick!"

As they darted through the kitchen, Trixie suddenly remembered the gaping hole in the dining-room. "I'd better put that picture back in place," she whispered. "If a photograph of that secret hiding place appeared in the papers and Jonesy saw it, he'd think Jim found the money and would never stop looking for him."

She raced back and slammed the big oil painting against the wall as the photographer climbed in through the living-room window.

"Who's there?" he called out as he heard the loud bang.

Trixie dodged through the pantry into the kitchen and drew Honey quickly behind her down the cellar stairs. She had left her flashlight in the alcove, so it was pitch black with the door closed.

"I'm too scared to move," Honey breathed. "We'll break our necks on these rickety old steps." She pitched forward then against Trixie and let out an involuntary scream.

Trixie groped wildly in the darkness for the railing and found it just in time to prevent both girls from falling to the stone floor below. "We've got to go down and hide behind something now," Trixie said desperately. "If he heard you scream, he'll open the door and find us on the stairs."

Somehow, they found their way down, and in the narrow shaft of light from the small, cobwebby window, they located the furnace and hid behind it. Just in time, too, because, in a minute, the kitchen door swung open, and a man's voice called out:

"Anybody home?"

A spider scurried across Honey's arm, and she had to set her teeth to keep from crying out. She let out a long sigh of relief when the man finally moved away, closing the door behind him.

They crouched behind the furnace, listening to the footsteps on the floor above for what seemed like hours. At last there was a long silence, and Trixie groped her way back up the stairs. With the additional light from the kitchen, Honey followed her, and together they tip-toed into the hall. From there they could see into both the dining-room and living-room and felt reasonably sure that the photographer had gone.

"He may be taking pictures of the outside," Trixie whispered. "I'll climb out and look around." A taxi was just pulling out of the driveway at the foot of the hill and Trixie called, "He's gone, Honey. Come on. Let's go home."

Reddy was waiting for them in the clearing, and then they saw Queenie, proudly marching from the underbrush, clucking to five little newly hatched chicks.

Reddy circled around them with great interest but kept at a safe distance.

"Oh, aren't they darling?" Honey gasped. "She's really a wonderful mother. I don't blame her now for flying at me the other day. I must have almost stepped on her nest."

Trixie chuckled. "Even Reddy has sense enough to stay away from her when she has chicks." She patted her pocket to make sure the ring was safe. "I'm glad we have something for Jim, anyway. And let's try to keep him from worrying the rest of the time. I can hardly wait for our ride tonight. Regan was swell to let us go."

"He said he wouldn't worry about us if Jim was along," Honey said. "But I had an awful time talking Miss Trask into letting me stay with you tonight. At first she wanted to come, too, or invite you up to our place."

"I was afraid of that," Trixie admitted. "How'd you ever make her give in?"

"I honestly don't know." Honey smiled. "She was arguing with me when suddenly she stopped in the middle of a sentence. 'Why, Honey Wheeler,' she sort of gasped, 'you're getting *fat!* And you're as brown as a berry. Your parents will be very pleased when they get back and see you looking so well.' And then she said, more to herself than to me, 'It's that Belden child that's done it,' and added, 'All right, Honey, you have my permission to spend the night with Trixie. As a matter of fact, there's a movie in the village I want very much to see. Regan will be here if you need him. I'll tell him to stay up till I get back.' "

"It's perfect," Trixie cried. "Now she'll be away from the house when we go for our ride."

Jim was asleep on the living-room sofa when they got back, but he awoke with a start when Trixie yelled, "Jim, look what we found! A diamond ring!"

He rubbed his eyes dazedly as he stared at the huge stone, and then he carefully examined the inside of the gold band. "It belonged to my great-aunt, all right," he said. "See, here are the initials and what was probably the date of their wedding. I hate the thought of selling it, but it'll keep me for a long time, in case I don't get a job right away." He grinned up at Trixie. "Well, you win. You did find some hidden treasure, after all."

"It was really Honey who found it," Trixie said generously. "It was her idea that there might be a wall safe behind that old painting."

Honey flushed with pleasure as Jim smiled his thanks. "This is one thing Jonesy won't get his greedy hands on," he said determinedly. "He can do what he likes with the money he gets from the sale of the property, but this belongs to me."

"I don't think he'll be allowed to touch that money," Trixie objected. "Not unless he can prove that he's supporting you."

Jim shook his head. "He'll get around that somehow. You don't know Jonesy."

Trixie and Honey fixed a delicious supper of frankfurters, rolls, salad, and chocolate milk shakes. It was almost nine o'clock when they finished talking, eating, and washing the dishes.

"You stay here, Reddy," Trixie said as she held the screen door open for the others. "Take good care of the house."

Reddy looked depressed but obediently lay down on the kitchen floor with his nose between his paws.

Trixie laughed as she let the screen door slam behind her. "That dog's so friendly he'd probably lead a burglar right to Mother's silver chest and help him cart it away."

"He certainly made friends with that photographer quickly," Honey said and then bit her lip as Jim asked, "What photographer?"

"Oh, nothing," Trixie said, trying to make her voice sound casual. "There was one up at the Mansion this afternoon, but he didn't stay long."

They were halfway across the lawn when Reddy,

pushing open the catch on the screen door with his nose, came bounding after them.

"Oh, look at this!" Trixie grabbed at Reddy's collar, but he leaped away and began running around them in circles, pretending that he'd known all along they were just playing a game and had no intention of leaving him behind. "He's a nuisance," she said when Jim finally caught him. "I'll have to lock him in. We can't take him with us. He'd chase everything in the woods and wake the dead with his silly barking."

Jim helped her drag the resisting Reddy back to the house. This time, Trixie locked the door and slipped the key into the pocket of her dungarees. "I hope he doesn't tear up the place out of spite while we're gone," she said. "He's never been left alone before. Mother always takes him with her in the station wagon when she goes shopping." They hurried across the lawn in the bright moonlight and started up the path to the stable. "He's nothing but a big, overgrown puppy," Trixie went on. "We all spoil him, and Bobby—" She stopped, rooted to the spot with horror, for the stillness was suddenly broken by the sound of crashing glass behind them, followed by the cry of an animal in pain.

Chapter 18
The Moonlight Ride

"Oh, oh," Honey gasped, "somebody's broken into your house and hurt Reddy."

At first Trixie thought something like that must have happened, and then as she turned she saw with relief that Reddy was bounding across the lawn.

"He must have gone right through a window," she said. "The only ones that aren't screened are the ones in Dad's study overlooking the terrace. He must have gone up there to watch us and then decided to jump out, even though the window was closed." Reddy dashed past them into the woods. "He's probably cut to ribbons."

"Not necessarily," Jim said. "I saw a policeman break through a window once without getting a scratch. Reddy might have broken a leg; but, from the way he's running, I'd say he was okay."

Trixie whistled and called, and finally Reddy came close enough to be caught and dragged back. From the terrace, Trixie pointed up to the shattered remains of the second-story window. "It's lucky our ceilings are so low," she said. "Otherwise he would have been badly hurt. I still can't believe he hasn't a cut, somewhere."

Inside the house, they examined him carefully but could not find a scratch. "We'd better put you in the cellar, old man," Jim said patting the dog affectionately. "It's a mean trick, but we won't be gone long."

Reddy was scratching and whining and snuffling on the other side of the door as they left the house for the third time.

"He's some dog," Jim said. "As soon as I get settled somewhere, I mean to get a pointer or a setter. You've never gone shooting with Reddy, have you, Trixie?"

"Brian and Mart do, sometimes," she told him. "But he isn't much good. Dad says we all tried to train him at once and that's what ruined him. Brian taught him to heel, Mart taught him to retrieve, and I taught him to come when called." She giggled. "You can see how well he obeys me, so you can imagine how good he is in other ways."

Regan was waiting for them with the three saddled horses. "I was just about to come down after you," he said. "Thought I heard the sound of breaking glass, but then I saw you coming across the lawn and figured you were okay."

He greeted Jim with a friendly, "Hi, youngster," just as though there was nothing unusual about his appearing with the girls. "Take good care of Jupe, won't you?"

"Yes, sir," Jim said. "It was swell of you to let me have one last ride on him."

"Going someplace soon?" Regan inquired as they mounted their horses.

"That's right." Jim rode off without another word.

In the woods it was cool and quiet except for the occasional *who, who-who, whooo* of an owl. Every now and then, they heard the bark of a fox off in the distance and the scurrying of small feet on the path ahead of them.

"This is heavenly," Honey sighed. "I thought I was going to be scared in the woods at night, but I'm not. It's much more fun and so much cooler than riding in the daytime."

"Dad used to take me on moonlight rides when I was just a kid," Jim told them. "Once I fell asleep on the way back, and he had to carry me on his saddle and lead my horse as well. Then, just as we got home, I woke up and yelled like anything because I'd missed so much fun." He chuckled. "Dad teased me about that for a long time."

"You loved your father an awful lot, didn't you?" Honey asked shyly. "You must miss him like anything."

Jim nodded soberly. "Guess that's why I hated Jonesy from the very beginning. I didn't think anyone could take Dad's place. I knew Mother needed someone to take care of her, but I wanted to do it. I was too young, of course." He cantered along the moonlit path in a thoughtful silence. "Sometimes I think if I'd behaved better at first, Jonesy might have been kinder to me. It's too late now, though. He hates me as much as I hate him. Once I looked up suddenly from my homework and caught him staring at me. There was such a mean look in his eyes that I was honestly scared to death for a minute."

Trixie swallowed hard, thinking of her own father who was always so cheerful and kind to everyone. *I never really appreciated him before,* she thought. *I'm always nagging at him to buy me this and buy me that when I know he can't afford it with four children to take care of.* She made a quick little resolution to reform and immediately felt much better.

After a while they reined in their horses beside a stream that was hardly more than a trickle. "Golly," Trixie said, "our brook's beginning to look like this. If it doesn't rain soon, all the wells will go dry."

Jim nodded. "That's one of the reasons why I had such a hard time keeping clean at Uncle James's. The well there *is* just about dry." He crumpled a leaf to a dry powder between his fingers. "It's much drier up here than it is across the road where we went riding yesterday. If a blaze started around here we'd have a regular forest fire."

The horses drank thirstily between the rocks in the shallow stream, and then Honey said, "We really ought to start back now. Regan said not to be gone more than an hour."

Forty minutes later, they had returned the horses and were about to start down the short cut to the hollow when Jim suddenly grabbed the girls' arms and pulled them off the path into the bushes. "There's someone up at the Mansion," he whispered, "and I think there's a car parked down at the foot of the driveway."

Trixie sucked in her breath. In the bright moonlight, she could distinctly see the head and shoulders of a man rising above the thicket. He was moving slowly and stealthily across the clearing, like a cat stalking its prey, and she felt a little shiver run up and down her spine.

"I'm sure glad we talked you into staying down at our place, Jim," she whispered. "That man's no reporter. You can almost feel how evil he is from here."

Trixie heard Honey gasp and felt the pressure of

her arm. "Let's go tell Regan," Honey begged. "We ought to stay at our house tonight, Trixie. I wouldn't dare go down into the hollow with that man's car parked so near your driveway."

"Honey's right," Jim interrupted. "You girls go back to the Manor House. I'm going to creep through the woods and see who that man is. If it's who I think it is—"

"Jonesy!" Trixie broke in excitedly. "You think it's Jonesy, don't you, Jim?"

He was standing in the long black shadow of an evergreen, but Trixie could see him nod his head. "He may have seen the New York papers this afternoon and driven right down the river after me. But I can't be sure until I get closer." He started off on the path that led through the woods to the Mansion, walking carefully and silently over the pine needles.

"Wait for me," Trixie cried impulsively. "If he should try to hurt you, I could hit him over the head with something. Don't go without me, Jim!"

"Okay." Reluctantly, Jim waited for her to catch up. "But don't step on a twig or make any noise that would warn him. I just want to see what he's up to."

"I'm coming, too," Honey said suddenly. "If things get bad, I can at least scream loud enough for Regan to hear us."

It took them much longer to walk along the trail than it had when they rode on horseback, and Trixie thought they would never reach the thicket around the clearing. Neither she nor Honey was as used to stalking in the woods as Jim was, and every time their feet disturbed a branch or a pebble, Trixie's heart momentarily stopped beating. Suppose Jonesy heard them and was waiting for them on the other side of the hedge? Suppose he had that big black whip in his hand that Jim often dreamed about? Maybe this was what Honey's nightmare and premonitions were all about.

At last, Jim pushed ahead of them through the thick vines and underbrush, and they crouched behind him, hardly daring to breathe. There was no sign of anyone in the clearing, and then they heard the faint crunch of gravel, and Trixie saw a thin, stoop-shouldered man coming around from the other side of the house.

"It's Jonesy, all right," Jim said, his mouth close to Trixie's ear.

The man peered through one of the front windows, and, as he turned away in the bright moonlight, Trixie thought she had never seen such a mean-looking face before. His thin lips were drawn back over yellow, protruding teeth; his eyes glittered cruelly. Long, muscular arms swung ape-like from his broad, bent shoulders; and she shuddered as she watched his thick, twisted

fingers light the cigarette which dangled from one corner of his ugly mouth.

He moved stealthily along, keeping close to the shadows of the house, and stopped suddenly beside the open living-room window. Trixie was sure she was going to hiccup or cough or sneeze as Jonesy hesitated for a moment, looking over one shoulder right at the spot where they were hiding. Then, with one more backward look, he silently swung over the window sill.

She could feel her breath hissing through her teeth as she crouched there, watching the glow of the cigarette as the man moved from room to room.

"My mug," Jim whispered desperately. "It's sitting right there on the mantel, and the Bible with the will inside is just beside it! Those catlike eyes of his will see them in the dark. He'll see everything!"

Oh, gosh, Trixie thought remorsefully. *Why did we forget to bring them down this afternoon?* She uttered a prayer of thanks that she had had the presence of mind to slam the big oil painting in the dining-room against the wall.

"Sh-h," Honey cautioned. "He's put out his cigarette. Now we won't know where he is."

In a minute or two, the broad, stooped shoulders of the man were silhouetted against the open window. He glanced cautiously around the clearing, then climbed out and thoughtfully stared up at the top floors as though debating whether or not he should search them before departing. Finally, after lighting another cigarette and with several backward glances at the old Mansion, he disappeared down the rutted driveway.

They waited breathlessly until they heard the motor of the car on the road below turn over, and then they stood up, stretching to watch it drive away toward the village.

"That settles it," Jim said as they moved into the clearing. "I'm going to stay up here tonight and keep an eye on this place."

"But, Jim," Honey objected, "suppose he comes back and catches you while you're asleep?"

"He won't," Jim assured her. "I'll sleep in the summerhouse. *If* I sleep." He vaulted in through the window and came back quickly with the mug and the Bible. "At least, he didn't take these with him. But he knows now that I've been living here." He lifted the overhanging vine which hid the entrance to the old arbor and began to crawl along to the summerhouse. "Good night, girls," he said. "You'll be perfectly safe down at Trixie's. He doesn't want to see you any more than you want to see him. Don't worry."

Reluctantly, Trixie and Honey started down the hill to the hollow. "He's crazy to try to sleep in that stuffy little house," Trixie complained. "But there's no sense in arguing with Jim. He's redheaded and stubborn."

The moonlight threw long black shadows across the path, and Honey edged closer to Trixie. "Do you think that awful man will come back?" she asked, tucking her arm through Trixie's as they came out of the woods behind the garage.

"I don't think so," Trixie told her. "At least, not tonight. Anyway, he won't bother us, as Jim said. He has no way of knowing that we're all alone in the house."

Chapter 19
The End of the Mansion

Honey shivered as they hurried across the moonlit lawn to the terrace. "I won't be able to sleep a wink. I'll dream all night of Jonesy's horrid face peering at me through that broken upstairs window. He looked so mean."

Trixie wasn't at all sure that she herself wouldn't have similar nightmares, but she forced herself to laugh as she unlocked the kitchen door and whistled to quiet Reddy's frantic barking. She let Reddy out for one last run, and then, at Honey's insistence, they locked all the downstairs doors and windows. By that time, they were so exhausted they fell into bed without bothering to brush their teeth.

In spite of her worries, Honey dropped off to sleep almost immediately, but Trixie couldn't close her eyes. Her whole body ached, but her imagination kept her thoughts whirling round and round, reenacting all the exciting events of the past week. She tossed and turned, trying to keep her face out of the bright path of moonlight which streamed in through the window, and finally she sat bolt upright in bed.

"It's no use," she told herself. "I just can't sleep. I'm too worried about Jim. He's not going to stay in the summerhouse. He's going to run away again tonight. I know he is. I could tell by the way he talked."

She slipped out of bed and tiptoed to the window to stare wide-eyed up at the old Mansion, sharply silhouetted against the starlit sky. "He won't dare stay there another minute now that Jonesy knows where he's been hiding." Hot tears welled up in her blue eyes. "We'll never see him again. If only that mean stepfather could have stayed away."

She rubbed away the tears which had momentarily blurred her vision. "Gosh," she whispered to herself. "I'm like Honey, seeing things. I could have sworn I saw a ghost floating out of that open living-room window."

She rubbed her eyes again. Something white and feathery was seeping up around the roof of the Mansion. As she watched, it disappeared into space, but then, as a puff of wind blew up from the hollow, she could see another pale, ghostlike form take shape on one side of the house.

It looks like ghosts, she thought with a nervous giggle. *I guess the moonlight's playing tricks on me, and I must be sleepier than I thought I was.* She turned to go back to bed when, with a start of horror, she remembered the glow of Jonesy's cigarette as he moved from room to room. "It's not a ghost," she cried out loud, wheeling back to the window. "It's smoke. Honey! *Honey,*" she shouted, sticking her bare feet into her loafers. "The Mansion's on fire!"

Honey opened her eyes sleepily and nestled firmly under the covers. Trixie reached across the bed and shook her shoulder. "Wake up," she yelled. "There's a fire up at the Mansion. It'll burn like anything with that junk in it. It might spread to the summerhouse before Jim could get out."

Honey scrambled out of bed, her hazel eyes wide with fright. Trixie pushed her toward the stairway. "Call the fire department right away while I go warn Jim. Hurry!" Trixie was unlocking the door to the terrace as she called this over her shoulder, almost stumbling over Reddy. As the door slammed behind her, she heard Honey at the phone, sobbing, "Operator! Operator! Fire! Fire! It's the big house at Ten Acres!"

Trixie raced up the driveway to the path, with Reddy at her heels. As she ran along, tripping and stumbling in her haste, she could plainly see gray-white puffs of smoke curling out of the open window.

"Jim," she screamed as she burst into the clearing. "Jim!"

And then she saw him, crawling sleepy-eyed, but alert, from the arbor. "The Mansion's on fire!" she got out. "Your stepfather's cigarette! All that trash! Jim!"

Instantly, he was wide-awake and through the window before Trixie could catch her breath. Then he reappeared again, almost knocking her down as she dragged herself over the sill. "It's that pile of old newspapers," he called out as he hurtled past her. "Stay where you are. I'll keep bringing cans of water. You throw them onto the fire."

Trixie choked in the smoke-filled room, and through her streaming eyes she could see that one pile of paper had burned to ashes and that the stack of magazines next to it was beginning to smolder. She threw can after can of water on it and only vaguely knew that Honey was now helping Jim, running back and forth from the almost dry well. The magazines, which were now a tower of flames, suddenly toppled forward and fell, showering sparks and bits of burning paper all over the room. One corner of the old mattress caught fire; and, coughing and choking, Trixie dragged it across the floor. Somehow, she managed to pull it out of the window and stamped out all the smoldering embers with her feet.

Through her streaming eyes, she saw Jim racing to the window with the watering can. He stopped suddenly and threw can and all through the window. "It's no use,"

he said, wiping his sweaty face with his arm. "The whole room is in flames. We can't stop it, now."

And then they heard the wail of sirens from the road below, mingling with the roar of the fire engines.

There was such utter confusion for the next hour that Trixie could never get the sequence of events straight. She would always remember the look of sheer desperation on Jim's face as he shot past her into the old arbor and how Honey had kept on bringing cans of water from the well long after the clearing was filled with firemen. She tried to warn Jim not to hide in the summerhouse, in case the fire should spread in that direction, which seemed likely, but nothing except a hoarse croak came out of her smoke-tortured throat. And all the while, in the back of her mind, she knew that the chemical truck was roaring up the rutted driveway. There was an awful moment of silence as the siren stopped screaming, and the motor of the truck stalled halfway up the hill.

And then there were firemen everywhere, working calmly under the direction of their chief. Trixie heard an order which had something to do with ventilation, and two firemen promptly raced up a ladder and began chopping holes in the roof. In a minute, they clambered down and reported that they could "feel the roof breathing from the pressure of the hot air under it."

She remembered the walled-up staircase then, and how all the other windows and doors were tightly closed. Even in her dazed state of mind, Trixie knew that the men were doing the best they could, but she realized the hopelessness of it all.

"They'll never save the house," she shouted at Honey through the uproar of the stifling flames. "But they've got to keep it from spreading to the woods. Your place and ours will go, then. There hasn't been enough rain lately."

Honey clutched her arm. "Oh, look. Isn't that Jonesy coming up the hill with all those people from the village who were here when the military plane crashed?"

Trixie wheeled around to face the driveway. Sure enough, leading the crowd of curious onlookers was the stoop-shouldered man. He stamped across the clearing, yelling at the top of his lungs to the fire chief, "My stepson's in there. Save him! Save him! He's the missing heir to the Frayne fortune. You must save him!"

"I think you're mistaken," Trixie heard the chief say quietly. "Mr. Frayne lived all alone, and he died recently. I assure you, my men have already made certain there is nobody in the house."

"Fool, fool," Jonesy howled, and Trixie knew that he

was in one of the insane rages Jim had described. "I was here earlier this evening and saw unmistakable signs that young Jim Frayne has been living here. He's being burned alive, I tell you. Put out the fire! Put out the fire!"

Maybe he does really care about Jim, Trixie thought as she started forward to tell the fire chief that Jim was safe, so that he would not send any of his men into the flaming house. At that moment the roof burst into flames, and the whole house collapsed in a blazing shower of sparks and burning chunks of wood.

Instantly, Jonesy's attitude changed. He danced up and down in fury, shaking his fists and screaming like a maniac. "You idiots! You lazy idiots! Half a million dollars was hidden in that house, and you've let it burn to the ground. A fortune wasted, you fools. Do you hear me? A fortune!"

It's the money he was worried about, not Jim, Trixie thought angrily. *I'm glad he thinks Jim was burned alive. Now he won't be likely to bother him any more.*

The firemen, paying no attention to Jonesy's hysterical accusations, kept right on working to keep the fire from spreading to the woods. When the last ember was extinguished, even Jonesy was forced to face the fact that there was nothing left worth salvaging. Whatever had been hidden in the Mansion had been completely destroyed by the all-consuming flames.

Screaming insults, the stoop-shouldered man turned away from the ruins and tottered down the driveway.

"Who was that?" a reporter asked the fire chief. "Sounded like a lunatic to me."

The chief laughed grimly. "They ought to keep people like that under lock and key. First he was yowling that his stepson was being burned alive and then he changed his tune. Said there was half a million dollars hidden in the place." He shrugged tiredly. "Never did believe that yarn about old man Frayne having a fortune hidden in this old house, did you?"

"Well, I don't know about that," the reporter said warily. "It has happened before, you know. Rich old recluses living in poverty. What was that about a stepson?"

"You know as much about it as I do," the chief said, in exasperation. "Your hysterical friend said young Jim Frayne, the missing heir, was being burned alive. That's all I know, and what's more, I don't believe a word of it." But the reporter was already hurrying down the hill after Jonesy and the villagers.

"Golly," Trixie gasped. "It'll be in all the papers tomorrow that Jim died in the fire. I hope that means Jonesy won't bother him any more. He's taken enough beatings."

247

She stopped short as she felt a strong hand on her shoulder and wheeled around, expecting to face Jim's stepfather.

It was Regan. "Don't you think you two have had enough excitement?" he demanded, grinning. "If Miss Trask ever finds out you were hanging around this place at this time of night—" He let out a long whistle. "I'm taking you girls home now," he finished firmly. "And see that you stay there the rest of the morning."

Meekly, the girls let him escort them to the Belden terrace where Reddy, who had scampered away when the roof of the burning house crashed to the ground, was impatiently waiting for them. The dog gave them a noisy welcome.

"What happened to that redheaded kid?" Regan asked as Trixie opened the door.

"He's all right," Honey said quickly. "But, please, Regan, don't let anybody know what you know about him. That horrible, old, stoop-shouldered man is his stepfather."

"Figured something like that," Regan said as he saw them safely into the house. "And don't you worry about me. I mind my own business, and I don't tell anybody anything that doesn't concern them." He strode away in the waning moonlight, humming softly to himself.

Chapter 20
The Missing Heir

Sunlight was streaming into the room when Trixie awoke the next morning, and she realized that she and Honey must have slept very late. Rolling on her elbow, she reached across to the other twin bed and poked Honey. "Wake up, sleepy head!"

"I am awake," Honey said, keeping her eyes tightly shut. "I've been trying to figure out for the past half hour whether it was all a nightmare or not."

"It was *not.*" Trixie swung out of bed. "Let's get dressed and hurry up the hill to see how Jim is." She sniffed. "Whew! My pajamas smell like smoke. Do yours?"

"Yes." Honey wrinkled her nose. "That's why I was pretty sure it wasn't a nightmare. Gosh, Trixie," she said as they washed and dressed, "I was awfully worried about Jim hiding out in the summerhouse last night when it looked as though the fire was going to spread to the woods. Weren't you?"

"I sure was," Trixie agreed. "And it's a good thing that place is practically all windows; otherwise the smoke might have made him pretty sick." She stopped in the kitchen long enough to scoop two oranges out of the refrigerator. "We can eat these on the way up," she said, handing one to Honey, "and have the rest of our breakfast later with Jim. Now that Jonesy thinks he died in the fire, maybe he'll stick around here a few days longer."

"Oh, I hope so," Honey said. "I wish Regan hadn't made us go home last night before we had a chance to see if Jim was okay."

"Well," Trixie said, grinning, "we were lucky it wasn't Miss Trask. She would have given us heck for going up there in our pajamas."

"I was so excited I didn't know what I had on," Honey said. "And I don't believe anyone else noticed, either."

"I planned to dress and go back and see Jim," Trixie admitted, "as soon as I was sure Regan was asleep. But I was so tired, the last thing I remember was toppling into bed." She stopped suddenly and flicked a strip of orange peel into the bushes. "Say," she said, trying to sound casual, "did you have a nightmare last night? The one about being in the sealed room with the big balloon pressing down on you?"

"Why, no." Honey stared at her in astonishment. "I haven't had that nightmare for a long time. As a matter of fact, except for that one about the big black snake with the white streak down its back, I haven't even dreamed since we moved up here."

Trixie chuckled. "Well, I bet you don't have that sealed-room dream any more. If ever you were going to have it, you would have last night. What with the fire and worrying about Jim, I'm surprised I didn't have a nightmare myself."

The air was strong with the smell of smoke and scorched wood as they pushed through the thicket into the clearing.

"I bet I don't have any nightmares any more," Honey said thoughtfully. "And it's a funny thing, but that creepy feeling I had that something awful was going to happen has gone away, too."

"I should think it would." Trixie laughed. "The awful thing has happened. Nothing could have been much worse than the fire!"

The girls whistled, "Bob *White!* Bob *White!*" over and over again, but there was no answering call from the hidden summerhouse. Reddy sniffed around the ruins with an air of disgust and ran off through the woods after a rabbit. It was terribly quiet in the clearing, for not even a chicken was in sight.

"He must still be asleep," Trixie said as they stood

there listening. "Jim," she yelled. "It's all right. Come on out."

There was no sound except the wind rustling the leaves of the trees and the distant rumble of thunder in the overcast sky. "Maybe he got smothered," Honey breathed. "There was so much smoke around here last night, and the windows of the summerhouse are choked with vines."

But Trixie was already on her hands and knees, crawling as fast as she could under the old arbor, calling, "Wake up, Jim! It's us, Trixie and Honey."

Honey followed after her so closely that when Trixie swung open the door to the summerhouse, she almost knocked her down. A spider scuttled across the bare floor.

"He's gone," Trixie wailed. "I was afraid he'd run away the first thing in the morning. Now we'll never see him again, Honey."

Honey's hazel eyes clouded with tears. "Oh, gosh," she cried, "why didn't he wait to say good-by? I hoped that, now he doesn't have to worry about Jonesy any more, he might come and live with us."

"Me, too," Trixie moaned. As her eyes grew accustomed to the semi-darkness, she suddenly spied a piece of paper on the floor of the summerhouse. It was held in place by the little leather jewel case. "It's a letter from Jim," she cried excitedly. "Help me pull away some of these branches, Honey, so we can read it."

A shaft of grayish light trickled through the gap in one of the windows, and Trixie and Honey read the letter.

Dear Trixie:

You and Honey are great sports, but this is good-by. I heard Jonesy yelling last night, and now that he thinks I'm dead my troubles are over.

But what do you think? Early this morning I tripped over that old mattress you dragged out of the house, and I guess that it must have been so trampled by the firemen that the ticking tore into shreds when my knees hit it. And then I saw that old mattress I'd been sleeping on every night was stuffed with money! Not half a million dollars but enough to keep me going for a long time. You were right. A treasure was hidden in the Mansion and in the very room where you said all along we'd find it.

As soon as I get settled somewhere, I'll come back and repay you two for all you've done for me. But in the meantime, I want you to have my great-aunt's ring to remember me by. After all, you found it, and you saved the money from the fire. If you like, I think you can sell it for enough to buy that horse you want so much.

Please, don't you and Honey forget me. I'll see you sometime.

Yours, Jim.

"Honey," Trixie said sadly, "he really has gone. We're going to miss him like anything, and I wouldn't think of selling this ring. I'll *earn* the money for a horse and keep this to remember Jim by. But we'll never forget him, will we, Honey?"

Honey shook her head. "Never, never. He was almost the nicest person I ever knew. And," she added slowly, "he called *me* a good sport, Trixie. Can you believe it?"

Trixie laughed. "What's so wonderful about that?"

Honey flushed. "Oh, I know it sounds silly to you, Trixie, but nobody ever called me that before. I never had any real friends till I met you and Jim."

Trixie put her arm around Honey's shoulder and hugged her impulsively. "Well, you've got me as your friend for as long as you want me, Honey. And I'll bet Jim does come back some day."

Honey smiled. "You know, I've got one of my funny feelings about that. I've got a sort of premonition that we're going to see him again. Soon." She stopped as a

man's voice on the other side of the hidden summer-house broke in.

"Hello! I can hear you two, but I can't see you. Where are you?"

For one frightening moment, the girls clung together, terrified that Jonesy might have come back. Then, as the man called again, "Hello there," they knew it was not Jonesy's voice.

Hastily they scrambled out under the arbor and almost bumped into a tall, well-dressed man with thick gray hair and a gray mustache.

"Hello," he said again. "I'm George Rainsford, the late Mr. Frayne's attorney." He smiled pleasantly. "Are you two real or are you wood sprites?"

It was Honey who regained her poise first. "Why, I know you," she said. "I'm Honey Wheeler. Matthew Wheeler's daughter. Didn't you come to our apartment in New York for dinner one evening last winter?"

Mr. Rainsford nodded and shook hands. "Yes, I did. But I certainly would never have recognized you. You must have gained about ten pounds since then, and you've acquired quite a tan."

Honey introduced Trixie. "We're neighbors," she said. "The Beldens live down in the hollow, and Dad bought the place on the other hill."

Mr. Rainsford sobered suddenly. "Then you two may be able to help me. I'm trying to track down young James Winthrop Frayne II. I stopped at a little store on the way up here, and the man there told me he'd seen a redheaded boy riding through the woods the other day." The girls gave each other quick, secret looks as Mr. Rainsford went on. "The morning papers in the city said that the Frayne heir was burned to death in the fire here last night." He smiled. "Somehow, I don't quite believe that. The Fraynes are too tough and too smart to be caught in a burning building."

Trixie decided to take the bull by the horns, then. Even if Jim didn't want anyone to know he was still alive, she knew she could trust this man, and that he would be a real friend to Jim.

"Jim wasn't caught in the fire," she blurted out. "He hid in the summerhouse, but then he ran away again."

"And you girls know where he is?" Mr. Rainsford said, with an encouraging smile.

Trixie shook her head regretfully. "No, we don't. He left a note, but he didn't say where he was going."

"How did you happen to meet Jim in the first place?" Mr. Rainsford asked.

"We came up here to explore the morning Dad took old Mr. Frayne to the hospital," Trixie told him. "And we found Jim asleep on the floor of the living-room."

Mr. Rainsford stared at her in surprise. "Do you mean to tell me you girls broke into the house? Didn't you know you were breaking the law?"

Trixie flushed. "We only went inside to lock up the place," she said quickly. "Honey saw a face at the window earlier, and I thought we ought to make sure it wasn't a tramp or someone from the village who knew Mr. Frayne was in the hospital. You see, there was supposed to be half a million dollars hidden in the house, and I—"

"And what if it had been a tramp or a thief?" Mr. Rainsford interrupted sternly. "An ugly fellow who might have done something unpleasant to prevent you from reporting him to the police?" He frowned. "It was very wrong of you and an extremely dangerous thing for you to have done. Why, even I, Mr. Frayne's attorney, wouldn't have entered the house without first obtaining a search warrant."

Trixie stared shamefacedly down at her shoes.

"We didn't mean to do anything wrong," Honey broke in. "We just didn't think."

Trixie grinned ruefully. "It's a bad habit I have— acting before I think."

Mr. Rainsford relented and smiled then. "I'm sure you meant well and that you'll never do anything like that again. Now, please, go on with your story. Your tramp turned out to be Jim?"

Trixie nodded and quickly told him everything that had happened, beginning with why Jim had run away from his stepfather.

When she had finished, Mr. Rainsford said slowly, "I suspected something like that. Actually, Jim has nothing to worry about from Jones. I've gathered enough evidence from neighbors on the farms outside Albany to prove to a judge that Jim's stepfather is not a competent guardian. As soon as we locate him, I'll take the matter to court and have another guardian appointed."

Trixie let out a sigh of relief, and Honey looked as thought she were going to dance up and down with happiness. Mr. Rainsford smiled at them. "Jim sounds like a great lad. I'd like to adopt him myself. Will you two help me find him?"

"Of course, we will," Trixie and Honey cried together, and Trixie added, "We've got some clues, Mr. Rainsford. He told us he was going to apply for a job at one of those three big boys' camps upstate."

"Well, that makes it easy, then," the lawyer told them. "And when we do find him, there's half a million dollars in trust waiting for him."

"Golly," Honey gasped. "Then Jim really is a missing

heir after all, and old Mr. Frayne wasn't a crazy miser."

"Not exactly," Mr. Rainsford explained. "Mr. Frayne got a bit queer after his wife's sudden death. He took all of his money out of banks and turned over the rest of his estate to me. He formed a trust for his great-nephew, but I was not to inform Jim of this trust until after his uncle's death." He frowned. "I wish that boy had got in touch with me before he ran off again. I'd better get right on the phone and start calling those boys' camps."

"Oh, don't do that," Trixie begged. "You don't know Jim. He's as stubborn as a mule. If he got the least bit suspicious that somebody was looking for him, he'd think it was Jonesy; and then he'd disappear for good. If he got a job on a cattle boat that was sailing right away, it might be years before we could locate him."

Mr. Rainsford looked at her sharply. "Well, what do you suggest then? He's not going to have an easy time getting a job at one of those camps without written permission from his parents or guardian. If we don't act quickly, he may ship aboard a cattle boat, anyway."

"We'll go and look for him, ourselves," Trixie cried. "Honey and I. He wouldn't worry at all if he heard two girls were trying to trace him. He'd know it was us and he trusts us, you see."

"But," Mr. Rainsford objected, "you two can't go

wandering around the state all by yourselves."

"It's a perfectly wonderful idea," Honey broke in, enthusiastically. "We'll go in our trailer. Daddy's got an enormous one which we almost never use, because Mother won't travel any way except by plane. It's really a darling little house on wheels. Oh, we'll have a wonderful time, won't we, Trixie?"

Mr. Rainsford's heavy gray eyebrows shot up, questioningly. "All by yourselves?" he repeated, and shook his head at them.

Honey's flushed face grew even redder. "Oh, no! Miss Trask, my governess, will go with us. She's a perfectly marvelous driver. Daddy is always saying that he feels safer with Miss Trask behind the wheel than he does when Regan's driving. Regan doesn't care about anything but horses," she explained with a laugh. She grabbed Trixie's arm. "Let's all go over to my place now," she cried. "If Mr. Rainsford helps us tell Miss Trask how important it is to find Jim right away, I'm sure she'll agree to the plan. *Come on!*"

Trixie chuckled inwardly as Honey impatiently led the way through the thicket to the trail that ran between the two estates. *Honey's worse than I am, now,* she thought. *Barging off in a great hurry, without even thinking about what might happen. I wonder what will happen on that trailer trip. Something exciting, I bet, if it has anything to do with Jim and Honey. Which it has!*

As though in answer to her thoughts, there was a sudden loud crash of thunder and a jagged fork of lightning streaked across the sky.

The long-awaited rain was coming down in torrents as the three of them hurried up the steps to the wide veranda of the Manor House where Miss Trask was anxiously watching for them.

Julie Campbell's Beloved Girl Detective Is Back!

Don't Miss These Trixie Belden Favorites Coming Soon!

Available wherever books are sold.